With everything arranged, Eric helped Marissa into the cart after she removed her other sandal and stuffed the shoes into her bag. Walking through the park with both heels had been hard enough, doing it with one shoe and a sprained ankle proved impossible.

Eric sat next to her and lifted her injured foot to rest across his leg. Marissa groaned silently at the sensations his touch sparked, feeling like a jerk for wanting what she couldn't have. To make things worse, she'd been right about him being as hard as he looked. Besides already having been caught against his firm chest and carried in his arms, now she could feel the solid muscle of his thigh beneath her calf. Another shiver shimmied along her spine when he left one warm hand resting on her shin and the other cradled her bare heel.

Maybe going off with him, without the girls, wasn't such a good idea. They seemed to be the only thing keeping her inappropriate attraction in check.

She reminded herself yet again, married men were always off-limits. *Always*.

"How're you doing?" Eric asked. "Is the pain still really bad?"

"It's okay," she answered honestly.

As Santa climbed into the driver's seat, Reese stepped up to the cart with a wide grin and tapped on her father's arm. At her insistence, Eric leaned down so she could whisper in his ear, but Marissa heard Reese's statement so clearly the little imp could've shouted the words.

"Daddy, you're under the mistletoe."

Praise for Stacey Joy Netzel's other titles:

"The **Romancing Wisconsin Series** is fantastic. While the stories are simple and easy to read, the characters are amazing and the plot makes you want to keep reading straight through to the end." ~ Debbie, Amazon reviewer, 5 Stars

"[**Evidence of Trust**] grabbed me from the beginning and I couldn't put it down. I loved Britt and Joel! I loved the action and the suspense and of course the romance!!" ~ Angie, Amazon reviewer

"**LOST IN ITALY**...starts off right away, and every page that follows is packed full of excitement that will keep you on the edge of your seat." ~ Danielle, The Book Whore Blog ~ 5 Hearts—Could not put down amazing

"From start to finish, **RUN TO ROME** held my attention and wouldn't let it go. It was one of those books that if someone interrupted me, they had something heavy launched at their heads. I finished it in only two days, that's how fun it was!" ~ Adria, Adria's Romance Reviews, 5 Stars—Fantastic

"Stacey Joy Netzel is at the top of her game with **CHASIN' MASON**. I was hooked at page one and stayed hooked until the end...you'll love it!" Becky ~ Dark Angel Reviews, 5 Stars

"I loved how Ms. Netzel penned **MORE THAN A KISS** to be a rags to riches theme and she did so in such a realistic fashion the readers walked away believing the situation as if it truly happened to real people. This is another satisfying story I think the readers will love!" ~ Diana Coyle, Night Owl Reviews, TOP PICK

Stacey Joy Netzel's Other Titles:

ITALY INTRIGUE SERIES
  Lost In Italy*
  Run to Rome
  Vanished in Venice
  *2012 Write Touch Readers' Award Winner

COLORADO TRUST SERIES
  Evidence of Trust
  Trust by Design
  Trust in the Lawe
  Shattered Trust
  Dare to Trust

WELCOME TO REDEMPTION SERIES
  A Fair to Remember, Book 2
  Grounds For Change, Book 4
  The Heart of the Matter, Book 6
  Hold On To Me, Book 8
  Say You'll Marry Me, Book 10
  (books 1,3,5,7,9 written by Donna Marie Rogers)

ROMANCING WISCONSIN SERIES
  Mistletoe Mischief
  Mistletoe Magic
  Mistletoe Match-up
  Autumn Wish
  Autumn Bliss
  Autumn Kiss
  Spring Fling
  Spring Serendipity

STAND ALONE ROMANCE TITLES
  More Than a Kiss, contemporary romance
  Chasin' Mason, contemporary western romance
  Ditched Again, high school reunion novella
  Dragonfly Dreams, Christmas novella

PARANORMAL ROMANCE TITLES
If Tombstones Could Talk
Beneath Still Waters (Part One)
Rising Above (Still Waters Part Two)

Best Wishes & God Bless! [handwritten]

Mistletoe

Mischief

Romancing Wisconsin
Book 1

Stacey Joy Netzel [signature]

BY

STACEY JOY NETZEL

This is a work of fiction. Names, characters, places, and incidents are either the product of the author's imagination or are used fictitiously, and any resemblance to actual persons living or dead, business establishments, events, or locales, is entirely coincidental.

Mistletoe Mischief, Romancing Wisconsin, Book 1

Copyright © 2012 by Stacey Joy Netzel
(previously published 2009 *Mistletoe Rules* Anthology)

Website and Blog: http://www.StaceyJoyNetzel.com
Facebook: Facebook.com/StaceyJoyNetzelAuthor
Twitter: http://twitter.com/StaceyJoyNetzel

Cover Design: Kim Killion

Print: ISBN-10: 1939143322
          ISBN-13: 9781939143327

Dedication

Donna and Jamie,
Thanks for all the plotting sessions.
I look forward to many more!

Chapter 1

A high-pitched squeal pierced Marissa Wilder's ears.

"Daddy! You came!"

Marissa spun around as her daughter's new best friend, Reese, streaked past and launched her little body into the arms of a tall man. He was dressed as if he'd just returned from a tour in Iraq. Combat boots, desert camouflage pants, and a white T-shirt that appeared a size too small for his impressive physique. Muscled biceps looked huge wrapped around the six-year-old's tiny back. The only thing off with the homecoming picture was the fact that instead of a military buzz cut, his dark hair was long enough to reveal a hint of natural wave.

"Hey, sweetheart. Wow, what a welcome. I just saw you last night."

The sexy deep voice matched the man's devastating smile to perfection. Its smooth texture flowed over Marissa, leaving a warm feeling in the pit of her stomach even though he wasn't talking to her. She glanced up at the blazing July sun, certain the temperature had risen a good ten degrees in the last twenty seconds. It certainly wasn't hot flashes at age twenty-nine.

Oh, good Lord—she'd been too long without a date! Besides the fact that usually in Northeast Wisconsin heat variances to that extreme went the other direction, the zoo was the last place to start fantasizing about brandy-flavored kisses and a rock-hard body. At least he *sounded* like he'd taste as satisfying as a well-aged brandy— and she just knew without a doubt he'd be as solid as he looked.

Heather gripped her hand tighter. Marissa looked down at her own daughter, jarred from her inappropriate daydream about a married man. A married man expecting another child, no less—she'd spoken to Reese's pregnant mother, Nina, while waiting to pick Heather up from school yesterday. Her gaze latched on Reese's father's left hand, found it bare, and narrowed in annoyance with the reminder that not all married men advertised their attached status.

She wondered if Heather compared her friend's loving embrace with her daddy to the casual wave she'd received from her own father last month. Marissa wished Ted would grow up and be a better dad for Heather, but until that miracle happened, it was up to her to let their daughter know how much she was loved. She smoothed her free hand over Heather's straight blond hair and hugged her close to her side.

Reese pulled her arms from around her father's neck and frowned. "Mom said you were taking me to school this morning. Where were you?"

Marissa realized this guy was one of the no-show parent chaperones who'd caused the summer school program director to beg her for help this morning. With three important projects waiting on her desk, Marissa had started to apologize until she caught Heather's hopeful expression from the corner of her eye. A mental recalculation of her own personal deadlines to align with the customers' allowed her to stay and Heather's jubilant smile was worth it.

But right now, Marissa tapped one high-heeled black sandal and waited for this man's response to Reese's question. He had to be close to her ex's age of thirty, and though he looked ten times better now than Ted had at age twenty, missing field trips, kindergarten promotion programs, and birthday parties was exactly the sort of thing her ex did on a regular basis. Just thinking about Heather's disappointed face when she blew out her birthday candles last week made Marissa's jaw tighten.

"Ease up, Sarge," Reese's dad said. "I'm here now, and I'm all yours for the rest of the day."

"All day?" Reese exclaimed, her pretty blue eyes wide. "You never stay all day."

"All day," he confirmed, setting her back on her feet and ruffling her dark, silky curls. Reese gave a loud whoop of delight.

He appeared well practiced at diverting his

daughter's disappointment. Either he lacked the imagination to come up with a good excuse, or he was too lazy. With Nina's grumbles from earlier that morning of the man's irresponsible ways echoing in Marissa's mind, her irritation flourished even as a small voice inside whispered, *at least he showed up*.

Reese ran the few feet back to Marissa and Heather. "That's my dad," she proudly declared. "Heather, we're both lucky today! Dad's staying all day!"

Marissa smiled down at the excited girl until a battered pair of black boots entered her line of vision. Her pulse sped up. Her gaze drank in camouflaged-clad legs, trim waist, muscled chest and finally met a pair of smiling, smoky gray eyes framed by thick, dark lashes. Her heart thumped hard.

"Hi." He extended his hand. "Eric Riley, otherwise known as Reese's Dad."

With the slide of his calloused palm against her softer one, the temperature rose another five degrees. She caught the faint scent of pine wood. From him, or had the scent released from the nearby trees in the July heat and carried to her on the slight breeze?

She swallowed hard and managed to say, "I'm Heather's mom."

He waited a beat before his gaze shifted to her side to focus on her daughter. "Hello—I'm guessing you're Heather?"

"Hi," Heather chirped.

He returned his attention back to Marissa with a wide grin. "Nice to meet you, Heather's Mom."

"Dad," Reese giggled. "Her name is Mrs. Wilder."

His grip on her fingers loosened, and a flicker of what looked like regret flashed in his eyes. "Mrs. Wilder."

Marissa pulled her hand away, feeling like an idiot. She was relieved yet oddly disappointed to be free of his warm, rough touch. Heather reclaimed her right hand, reminding her of their surroundings. Other parents and children strolled past them at this very moment. She raised her other hand to brush at a wayward strand of blond hair that had become glued to her glossed lips. "It's Marissa."

His gaze followed her hand down to her side.

Then she felt the sweep of his gaze over her tan skirt and sleeveless black blouse on its way back up to meet her eyes.

"Pretty," he murmured, the gray of his eyes a shade darker.

Did he mean her name…or her? A flirtatious smile lifted the corners of his mouth. Marissa flushed so hot she had to fight the urge to fan her burning face. Yep, three years was definitely too long without a date.

In the next instant, she stiffened. What was she doing? The man was married for heaven's sake! And she'd just met him! A little harmless flirting among established friends may be no big deal, but this felt like something Ted would've done. *Had done,* one too many times.

Marissa looked pointedly at her watch and did her best to ignore Eric Riley. "Well, girls, we have about an hour to finish the scavenger hunt before it's time to feed the giraffes."

"Oh, oh, I wanna feed the giraffes! Can I, Mom? Please?" Heather bounced up and down, jerking on Marissa's hand every time her feet hit the ground. From alongside her father, Reese mirrored her friend's movements.

"Me, too. Me, too!"

It was impossible not to smile in the face of their exuberance. "Miss Patti assured me everyone gets to feed Larry and Lucy."

"Yay!" The two girls grinned at each other before running ahead to the next zoo enclosure that housed the raccoons. Marissa pulled their alphabet score sheets from her bag and started after them as fast as her high-heeled sandals allowed. She'd had a heck of a time keeping up with their endless energy all morning.

"Me, too?" Eric Riley teased, falling into step beside her.

His deep, seductive voice made her stomach flutter, so she purposely cast him an annoyed glance. The sight of him easily matching her hurried steps with long, confident strides didn't help her awareness or her ire. What she wouldn't give for a pair of her beloved tennis shoes right now.

She thrust Reese's paper at her father without saying a word. His brows rose in surprise at her outright rudeness, but he accepted the paper and perused it. When they reached the raccoon exhibit, Marissa had Reese read the display out loud, and then she asked a few questions about raccoons based on what they'd just learned. After they'd answered, the girls wrote 'raccoon' in the box for the letter R.

"What's with the Christmas lights and holly everywhere?" Eric asked on their way to the porcupine habitat.

Her gaze swept over numerous large candy canes and randomly placed decorated trees. If you asked her, Christmas belonged in December. With a mental eye-roll at the decorations and an inward sigh that she'd have to at least make small talk to avoid appearing like a total bitch, she explained briefly, "Christmas in July. After lunch they're having reindeer wagon rides and a visit with Santa."

"Oh, cool. The kids will love that."

The smile in his voice made it sound like *he'd* love that. She risked a glance, found him watching her, and stumbled on the uneven pavement. *Gol-darn heels.* Eric caught her arm and steadied her, his lightning fast reflexes somewhat stunning.

"You okay?"

"Yes, thank you." The huskiness in her voice

contradicted her efforts to ignore the tingle of awareness that radiated from his hand, up her arm, and into the rest of her body.

"Don't mention it." Then he ruined his chivalrous act by smiling down at her aching feet. "Tennis shoes might've been a better choice for a field trip."

Marissa pulled free of his grasp and stalked toward the porcupine enclosure where the girls waited. *Condescending jerk.* Went right along with the couple snide looks a few of the mothers had given her—like she'd purposely dressed up in a skirt and heels for the trip just to get attention. Trouble was, if she tried to explain her clothes and impractical sandals to Eric now, suppressed frustration would raise her voice, and she didn't want to do that in a public place, not to mention in front of the girls.

She held her temper, put a hand on each of the little shoulders in front of her, and waited for Heather and Reese to find the ball of quills underneath a log on the side of the concrete-enclosed area. This time Heather read the display, Eric jumped right in and interjected with two questions about porcupines, and the girls added to their sheets. Onward they went to the lynx cage, then the wallabies, and the river otters.

Reese's father continued to participate and Marissa had to fight a frown more than once at the silly questions he came up with.

"Wonder how they'd do on a trapeze?"

"Daad, it said otters are underwater acrobats."

It didn't help that though the girls seemed to have been having fun before Eric arrived, now they were having a ball.

On their way to the monkey cages, when the girls ran ahead again, he asked, "You said we had an hour to finish these?"

"Yes."

He leaned until his shoulder brushed hers and indicated another group of parents and kids walking a few feet away from them. Pine scent flirted with her senses again. Although he stood too close to risk direct eye contact, Marissa caught the frown on his face from the corner of her eye before he said in a low tone, "They're all done already."

He might as well have stated she was taking

too long. His apparent criticism of how she handled the scavenger hunt, coupled with his earlier comment about her shoes, put her simmering annoyance over the edge. She stopped dead in her tracks and planted her hands on her hips when he faced her. A deep breath helped her tone down the volume of her response.

"Of course they're done," she ground out. "Their kids ran from cage to cage without taking the time to read anything. I'd rather the girls only get half of it done and learn something about the animals we see than finish the hunt without learning anything new at all."

His brows rose, along with his hands. "I only meant to—"

"Next time you want to do it *your* way, try showing up on time."

Chapter 2

*E*ric snapped his slack jaw closed when Marissa Wilder swept past him in a huff. *Wow.* Someone had a major attitude, and she'd decided to direct it at the bull's-eye he must be wearing on his chest.

The sultry scent of vanilla lingered in her wake, continuing the relentless seduction his senses had ineffectively dealt with over the past hour. He'd had a feeling he was in trouble the moment he saw the woman his daughter had been laughing with when he arrived. In the looks department, the tall, leggy, blue-eyed blond was the exact opposite of his Italian-descent ex-wife, but they matched each other with their tempers, and their ability to get pissed off at him with a simple misinterpreted sentence.

Or in this case, probably two.

He'd been teasing her about the shoes, even though he was genuinely curious what possessed her to wear such sexy sandals to chaperone a field trip, and the comment about the scavenger hunt had been intended as a compliment. He liked that she didn't race the kids through the project like many of the other parents seemed to have done. Not making the extra effort to teach is exactly what Nina would've done—in addition to wearing something guaranteed to attract as much male attention as possible.

Marissa's slim-waisted, flowing, knee-length tan skirt and v-neck, sleeveless black blouse definitely garnered their share of attention from a number of men in attendance, yet since Eric arrived, she'd focused solely on their two girls—with the exception of a few words tossed toward him when he'd asked a direct question. Was she truly oblivious to the interested looks directed her way?

Eric stuffed Reese's half-completed score

sheet in his back pocket and followed the three girls to the giraffe exhibit. If Heather's mom was aware of the male attention, she did a heck of a job of ignoring them all—including him. When he'd openly flirted with her on his arrival, there'd been a moment when she'd been receptive. She let him hold the handshake a few heartbeats longer than necessary, her cheeks flushed, and when she spoke, her voice had that slight breathless quality that told him he wasn't the only one affected.

His pulse raced with excitement until Reese called her *Mrs.* Wilder and reminded him he had no business hitting on a married woman. Thank goodness her bare left ring finger quickly put him back at ease. If only it'd done the same for her. She shut him down before he could get past *hello* and move on to getting to know her.

Although one of the most important things was clear, she loved her daughter. For real—not because a judge or social worker watched her Mother of the Year performance. Any time Marissa hugged her cute-as-a-button miniature look-a-like, she never once glanced around to see who caught the touching show. She was just as wonderful with Reese, too.

Reese giggled with Heather, and Eric's chest tightened. Despite everything Nina had put them through the last year and a half, his little girl still smiled. He prayed with all his heart she stayed like that forever and didn't pick up any of her mother's less desirable traits.

If only he'd been able to win more time with her in the custody battle. Familiar frustration and resentment rose up at the thought of Nina's lawyers and friends dragging everything out into the open in court. They hammered home the fact that he worked *a lot*, either on call as a volunteer First Responder, or building his carpentry business. The kicker was, the only way Nina had gotten the alimony she needed to afford her custody lawyer was *because* he'd worked his tail off to establish his business.

It'd taken some time to get over his bitterness, but he could now admit the divorce wasn't completely Nina's fault. He took responsibility for burying himself in his work when the marriage started to go south, and then he spent even more time in his workshop when he found out about her affair. And a good father would've been around more for Reese when she needed him.

That guilt would never completely ease. But at least his current efforts to make up for his mistakes were paying off. His older brother's platoon had returned safely from their second tour in Iraq, and once Mark ended his Term of Service and moved back home come November, there'd be more volunteer First Responders to cut back on Eric's on-call days. Better yet, his woodworking reputation had reached a place where he could charge higher prices for the elaborate pieces and work less hours, freeing him up to spend more days like today with Reese.

Everything was in place for him to re-petition for joint custody at the hearing scheduled in August. With Nina remarried, and now almost five months pregnant, he just wasn't so sure which direction she'd swing. Hopefully he'd proven he could be depended on for more than just money. As tired and moody as she'd been lately, he prayed she'd be receptive to him dealing with Reese's energy for half the time instead of just every other weekend.

"Daddy, come on! We have to get in line," Reese called, curving her little arm in an arc for him to hurry up.

He smiled and increased his stride to catch up, anticipating a similar expression on her face at home later when she saw he'd finished the tree house in the backyard. He'd bought marshmallows too, so they could make s'mores at the campfire before climbing up to sleep amongst the leaves. It'd been far too long since they'd done something like that.

He took the steps two at a time to stand behind the girls on the raised platform that put zoo-goers at eye level with the fourteen-foot tall giraffes. An accidental brush of his arm against Marissa's made him feel more alive as a man than he had in over a year. The awareness coursing through him convinced him not to give up the chase just yet, even if her sideways glance remained less than encouraging.

Reese bounced on her toes in front of him. "I need a quarter so I can get some crackers for Lucy."

Eric dug into his pocket. Before his fingers

could scrape up his loose change, Marissa held out her hand to Reese. "Here you go, honey. There's two for both you and Heather."

"Don't forget Larry," Eric called after his daughter. That earned him an eye roll from Marissa, but hey, someone had to look after the guy. He hesitated, and then stepped in front of her, because sometimes, the *guy* had to look after himself. After a quick scan to assure semi-privacy, he moved closer so she'd be the only one to hear his low-pitched voice. "Listen— about what I said—"

She leaned sideways to see past him. "Heather, Reese, stand back and wait your turn."

Eric checked over his shoulder to see the two girls alongside the fence surrounding the platform, their rye crackers in hand. They looked fine, so he faced Marissa again. This time she lifted her blue gaze direct to his. His pulse revved like his circular saw just before it bit into a plank of fresh pine.

"Forget it," she said. "I overreacted."

"If I'd meant it the way you took it, you'd have been justified," he allowed. "But I was trying to point out it was good you were going so slow."

"Oh." Her gaze flickered from his, and she glanced around his shoulder again. "Heather, get down off the railing. It's almost your turn."

Eric shifted to keep an eye on Reese and continued the conversation. "I like that you took the time to teach them at each—"

He broke off when Reese reached up to tickle Heather, who'd leaned over the top of the fence to see the giraffes better. Heather wobbled precariously before tipping the wrong direction with a terrified shriek. His heart about stopped beating at the same time he heard Marissa gasp in panic beside him.

"Heather!"

He didn't remember pushing past the other people on the platform to cross the distance between them and the fence, all he knew was he caught the little girl at the last second before she plunged head first onto the concrete twelve feet below. He clutched her tight against his thundering chest. Sobs shook her slim little body while her hold on his neck choked hard.

"Shh. I got you sweetheart. You're okay," he

soothed. Concerned voices began to bleed back into his consciousness.

"I want my mommy," Heather cried into Eric's T-shirt.

He turned to find Marissa at his side. She dragged her daughter from his arms to crush her close. Tears ran unchecked down both their faces.

"I was so scared, Mommy."

"So was I, honey, so was I. But you're safe now." Marissa's voice shook worse than the hand she stroked over her daughter's hair.

Reese stood off to the side, looking pretty frightened herself. Eric scooped her up and hugged her close. Just the thought of his daughter facing such danger chilled him to the bone.

Marissa's radiant blue gaze met his over Heather's shoulder. "Thank you," she said softly.

Reese burst into tears and burrowed against his neck. Eric frowned and tried to see her face. "Hey, what's the matter? Everything's okay."

After another moment of crying, Reese calmed down enough to mumble, "It's my fault." Then she lifted her head to look at Heather, who peered shyly from under Marissa's chin. "I'm sorry I tickled you, Heather."

"Oh, honey, no one blames you," Marissa exclaimed. She stepped closer and rubbed Reese's back. "It was an accident."

Reese wiped her eyes before drying her hand on Eric's T-shirt. She sniffed and laid her head on his shoulder while peering at her friend. Heather's tremulous smile melted Eric's heart as much as his daughter's obvious remorse.

"I'm not mad," Heather said.

"So we can still be best friends?" Reese asked in a tiny, hopeful voice.

Heather nodded.

"I'll never tickle you ever again," Reese promised, solemnly.

"And no one climbs up on the railings again, either," Marissa added, her tone firm. "Okay?"

Both girls nodded. Moments later, they wiggled for freedom. Eric exchanged a relieved smile with Marissa before they both set their daughters down. Heather headed straight for the fence, prompting Marissa and Eric to both make mad grabs for her shoulders. Marissa caught her, but not before Eric noticed a tight grimace of pain cross her face with her shift in stance.

"I lost my crackers." Heather sniffed, peering down over the edge at the scattered crumbs on the concrete.

"You can have mine." Reese held both crackers out to her friend.

Heather grinned but only took one. "We'll share."

They promptly got back in line and waited their turn to feed the giraffes. Expelling a breath to release the tension in his shoulders, Eric shook his head in disbelief. To be the child and not the parent; sure she'd just had a near-miss, but heaven forbid she miss her chance to feed Lucy.

While Marissa spoke to a couple of the parents and one of the platform attendants who wanted to make sure everything was all right, Eric bought more crackers and divided them evenly between the two girls before returning to her side. He felt they'd bonded somehow, and leaned against the railing while she snapped pictures of the girls feeding the giraffes. Excited smiles lit up their faces when the huge animals took the crackers from their small hands.

"Can you believe those two?" Eric asked after she'd snapped a few photographs.

"I know," Marissa agreed. "Like nothing even happened, while I'm still recovering from my heart attack."

Emotion clogged her voice. She held out a still-trembling hand to show him the lingering after-effects of the scare. Eric reached to take hold of her fingers and squeezed gently with reassurance, knowing exactly how she felt. As he rubbed his thumb back and forth across her knuckles, fresh tears brightened her eyes and an overwhelming urge to gather her close for a comforting hug surprised him.

"I don't even know how to thank you," she said.

"It could just as easily have been Reese. All that matters is that Heather's safe."

The girls rushed back to their side of the platform. Eric reluctantly released Marissa's hand as Heather asked, "Did you see me, Mom? Lucy licked me!"

Marissa blinked a few times before giving

her daughter a bright smile. "I got a picture of it," she said.

"Let me see!"

Both Reese and Heather crowded close to view the digital camera screen, giggling over Lucy's tongue and themselves in the snapshots. Reese pulled Eric close to see a picture of her with her hand near the mouth of one of the giraffes. "That's Larry, Dad. I didn't forget him."

Eric grinned and ruffled her dark curls, surprised she'd remembered. "Atta girl. So, what's next?"

"Lunch!" they exclaimed in unison and took off for the stairs.

"Hey, slow down and wait for us," Eric called before raising his brows toward Marissa. She didn't seem in her usual hurry to tail the kids. "Ready?"

He started forward, but with Marissa's first step, she gasped in obvious pain. She lifted pressure off her right foot so fast that any amount of balance she had on her left was lost. Eric ducked one flailing arm and caught her against his chest before she went down.

Chapter 3

"Whoa—what the heck did you do?"
Eric's voice rumbled in his chest against her back, but Marissa was too busy biting back a whimper of agony to enjoy the feel of the strong arms that'd caught her.

"My stupid heel wedged in the boards before, and I twisted my ankle when Heather almost went over the railing."

And with that one single step just now, the throbbing pain she'd been trying to will away exploded into a thousand sharp knives stabbing at her ankle. Adrenaline had kept her oblivious until after she held Heather safe in her arms, and then, she'd hoped the pain would fade if she gave it a few minutes.

Obviously not.

"Mom? What's the matter?"

Heather stood in front of them with an anxious expression. Marissa wiped the moisture from her eyes and gave her daughter a reassuring smile. "I hurt my ankle a little, but it's okay, I'll be fine."

The knives had dulled slightly, receding enough to let the details of Eric's hard, muscular body register on her consciousness. He helped her straighten, and her body slid up along his chest in the process. A wave of heat crashed over her.

"Can you stand?" he asked.

"As long as you don't let go." The moment the breathless words escaped, her cheeks flamed. She sounded as turned on as she suddenly felt. Their daughters stood three feet away, for heaven's sake! Staring at their parents with big, round eyes.

"I won't let go," Eric promised. "Take a couple slow, deep breaths and I'll carry you to that bench down there."

Marissa focused her gaze toward the bottom of the steps. *Thank God.* He thought her breathlessness stemmed from the pain. A few moments ago, *yes*. Now? *Not so much*. And no way she'd let him carry her.

"I can walk."

"It'll be easier if—"

The zoo employee who'd checked on Heather earlier had noticed their group again. "Is everything okay?" the young man asked. "Should I call for the medical cart?"

"That's not a bad idea," Eric said. "Thanks."

"I'll walk," Marissa insisted when the employee lifted his walkie-talkie.

"Fine, you walk," Eric relented. But then he still nodded to the employee to make the call before stooping slightly to fit his shoulder under hers. His arm curved around her waist for support. "Let's go. Girls, wait for us at the bottom."

With his help, Marissa hobbled toward the stairs. She didn't know which was worse, her unsteady balance in the strappy sandals, or the riot of sensations radiating from his large hand spanning her waist. In an attempt to gain some equilibrium, she put weight on her right foot again. Pain attacked with a vengeance and she sucked her breath through her teeth.

A low growl of annoyance sounded deep in Eric's throat. "I need to look at your ankle sooner rather than later, and at the rate we're going, it'll take you a half hour to get down the stairs. Now hang on."

He scooped her into his arms, leaving her no option but to cling to his neck. At five feet seven inches without shoes, she must weigh three times what his daughter did, yet he strode down the platform steps as if she were as light as his six year old daughter.

"What possessed you to wear heels to the zoo anyway?" he muttered.

She stiffened in his arms. "I'll give you two guesses. One, I'm an airhead who enjoys people looking at her like she's an idiot. Or two, I was supposed to work today, ran late and missed the bus at school, drove Heather here to meet her class where Patti begged me to help because three of her chaperones didn't show up and after one look at my daughter's face, I knew I couldn't disappoint her." She took a much-needed breath of air. "So I stayed in my stupid high heels."

He'd descended the stairs and stood by the bench by now, but made no move to set her down. A slight frown creased his tanned brow.

Marissa lifted her eyebrows when his guilty gray gaze met hers. "Any other questions?"

"No."

He set her on the bench before kneeling at her feet. His deft fingers made short work of unfastening her sandal strap. He eased it off her foot, and she reached to take the shoe, ridiculously glad she'd splurged on a pedicure two days ago.

"Your ankle is swelling already," he noted, resting her bare foot on his camouflaged thigh. His work-worn hands were gentle and warm against her sensitive skin. A shiver raced along her spine at the sensual sensations his touch sparked. What did he do for a living to put those calluses on his hands?

His darkened gaze rose to hers. "This is going to hurt, and I'm sorry, but I have to feel for any obvious breaks. Ready?"

She nodded, a little nervous, yet at the same time, impressed by the calm confidence in his voice. Heather scooted onto the bench next to her on one side, and Reese took the other. Like curious little kittens, both of them watched every move Eric made.

Marissa did her best to endure the prodding without complaint, but couldn't control a couple of flinches and a swift reflexive jerk at one particular sharp stab of pain. Heather took hold of her hand, and Marissa smiled down at her through gritted teeth.

"You seem to know what you're doing," she said to Eric in an effort to distract herself.

"Daddy's a Pear Medic," Reese announced.

"Par-*a*-medic," Eric corrected without shifting his attention from his work. "I spent six years as a field medic in the Army, and now I'm a volunteer First Responder."

Ah ha. That explained his take-charge attitude, his determination to keep going after yet another gasp from her, *and* his hair. She'd thought it was a little long for him to be active-duty military. *That's right, focus on something other than the pain.* She stared at his bent head. Were those waves as soft and thick as they appeared?

Bet his wife wouldn't appreciate her finding

out any more than she had when Ted ran around. Marissa readjusted her gaze and refused to let it wander from the watch on his wrist.

"What's a first reponderer?" Heather asked.

This time, Eric glanced up. "Responder. I help people who are hurt until the paramedics arrive to take them to the hospital."

Finally, he rested her foot on his leg again. "I don't think it's broken, but we'll need to get you to the ER for an X-ray to be sure. There could be a hairline fracture that I can't feel."

Heather clutched her hand in a death grip, lifting wide, frightened eyes to Marissa. "You have to go to the hospital?"

Marissa quickly shook her head. "Of course not, honey. Eric said it's not broken."

"You really need—"

She shot Eric a quelling look before catching sight of the summer school director over by the lion exhibit. "Oh, look, girls, there's Miss Patti. Could you go get her for me, please?" The moment they were out of earshot, Marissa turned back to Eric.

"You need an X-ray," he insisted before she could speak.

"I know," she agreed quietly. "But my ex's mother passed away last fall, and ever since then Heather's been afraid of hospitals. I'll go, but not with her. I can maybe see if Ted could take her tonight, or figure out something tomorrow."

The chances of Ted being available *and* willing to help were slim to none, so she considered her options for Saturday.

"You can't wait until tomorrow," Eric said with a frown.

Marissa bit back her argument when Patti, her three charges, and Heather and Reese arrived. "Good to see you made it, Eric," Patti said.

"Yeah, I'm sorry I missed the bus this morning, but better late than never…I think."

When he glanced up at Marissa with a crooked smirk, she knew he was referring to her little shoe tirade a few minutes ago. She couldn't help a small smile in return. The man was much too handsome and boyishly charming for his own good, and she never had been very good at holding a grudge—especially with him being so nice about her ankle. The warmth tingling up her leg from the touch of his hands on her foot melted her resistance even more.

A wimpy beep broke their moment of connection. She turned to see a golf cart had pulled up to the bench, candy cane striped with holly boughs strung across the front. When the driver stepped onto the pavement, Marissa covered her mouth to smother a laugh of disbelief. She may not care for all the Christmas stuff in the middle of summer, but this was priceless. The kids giggled without reservation.

"*Ho, ho, ho.* One of my helpers told me someone's lookin' fer a ride over here."

Santa stood before them, unlike any St. Nick Marissa had ever seen. He wore his white-ball topped hat, had the required wire-rimmed glasses perched on his nose, a long, white beard and rosy cheeks, and a big ol' belly…but that's where the similarities ended.

"Daddy, where's Santa's pants?" Reese whispered loud enough for everyone to hear.

Indeed, Santa's pants and white trimmed red jacket were hilariously absent. In their place, red suspenders bulged over a white T-shirt, holding up a pair of cherry-red shorts. Matching red flip-flops completed the outrageous outfit.

Santa waggled his bushy white eyebrows at the kids. "It may be Christmas in July, but this here ain't the North Pole, you know. I should get a vacation, too, don't you think?" After they nodded their agreement, he turned to Eric and Marissa. "How ken I help?"

"A ride to the first aid office would be great," Eric said, gently setting aside Marissa's foot before rising to his feet.

"I'll take Heather and Reese with us to the South picnic area," Patti offered before Marissa could even ask.

Marissa hugged Heather, who'd come back to stand next to her with a worried expression. "We should be back in time for the reindeer wagon rides. Until then, you be really good for Miss Patti, okay?"

"I will," Heather promised solemnly. Reese nodded as well.

Patti smiled. "The two of them are always good. And I'll make sure to save you each a plate for lunch."

With everything arranged, Eric helped Marissa into the cart after she removed her other sandal and stuffed the shoes into her bag. Walking through the park with both heels had been hard enough, doing it with one shoe and a sprained ankle proved impossible.

Eric sat next to her and lifted her injured foot to rest across his leg. Marissa groaned silently at the sensations his touch sparked, feeling like a jerk for wanting what she couldn't have. To make things worse, she'd been right about him being as hard as he looked. Besides already having been caught against his firm chest and carried in his arms, now she could feel the solid muscle of his thigh beneath her calf. Another shiver shimmied along her spine when he left one warm hand resting on her shin and the other cradled her bare heel.

Maybe going off with him, without the girls, wasn't such a good idea. They seemed to be the only thing keeping her inappropriate attraction in check.

She reminded herself yet again, married men were always off-limits. *Always*.

"How're you doing?" Eric asked. "Is the pain still really bad?"

"It's okay," she answered honestly.

As Santa climbed into the driver's seat, Reese stepped up to the cart with a wide grin and tapped on her father's arm. At her insistence, Eric leaned down so she could whisper in his ear, but Marissa heard Reese's statement so clearly the little imp could've shouted the words.

"Daddy, you're under the mistletoe."

Chapter 4

*E*ic bit back a grin at his daughter's keen observation. He glanced up at a sprig of leaves and holly berries attached to the roof of the cart, then dropped his gaze to Marissa's. "So we are," he murmured.

Her face flushed, but he couldn't tell if it was from embarrassment, or anticipation of a kiss. He knew the reason *his* pulse raced like an out of control locomotive.

"You have to kiss her," Reese stated.

God Bless you, Reese.

Santa laid his arm across the back of the front passenger seat and craned his head around, his brown eyes twinkling. "'Tis tradition."

"It's the *rule*," Reese argued, frowning at

Santa before turning back to Eric. "You say so every Christmas when we stand in the doorway at Grandma's."

"I do, don't I?"

Reese nodded emphatically. "Every year."

Eric faced Marissa and sighed with exaggerated reluctance. "I might've been able to buck tradition, but a rule's a rule."

He wondered what she'd do, especially considering the pressure of everyone watching. She cast a quick glance around at their audience, and then lowered that lovely blue gaze of hers to her lap. Despite the spitfire attitude he'd witnessed all morning, her hesitation hinted at a shy side, captivating him even more.

"I'm sorry," she finally said quietly. "But I can't help wondering what your wife would think of this."

Her disapproving words took him by surprise. *So much for shy.*

Then he considered her response. She thought he was still married? Talk about unexpected. Relief followed pretty fast when it dawned on him that maybe this was the reason she'd given his flirting the cold shoulder. He respected that she would honor the vows of marriage, even if it weren't her own.

Moving closer, he slid his ring-less left hand across the back of the seat to rest just shy of her shoulder. He spoke as low as she had, for her ears only. "Seeing as how my *ex*-wife is now married to the man she cheated on me with, I don't really give a damn what she thinks."

Her gaze rose, comprehension widening her expressive eyes. "Oh."

He leaned another few inches closer and whispered, "No girlfriend to worry about, either." Might as well lay it all out. He didn't worry about her being involved with someone, otherwise that would've been the first reason she gave to avoid the kiss.

Santa tooted the cart horn, making them both jump. "Today, folks. I got reindeer to hitch up."

Eric lifted a brow in silent question. Marissa wet her lips and offered a slow smile that sent his pulse into overdrive again.

"I've never been very good at breaking rules," she admitted.

Eric threaded his fingers through her soft hair

at the back of her neck and urged her forward. Her walnut-colored lashes lowered, fanning against her cheeks. He waited a moment, his mouth hovering above hers while he took in her natural beauty. At last, he closed the remaining inch between them.

Reese's giggle and their audience's applause kept Eric from slanting his mouth over Marissa's to take advantage of her surrender. What he wouldn't give to be completely alone with her for this first kiss.

He softly brushed her lips with his once, twice. A frustrating brief second of increased pressure to let her know he definitely wanted more, and then he reluctantly lifted his head. *Damn.* If he had anything to say about it, the next one would be longer, deeper, ten times hotter—and minus about seven or eight pairs of prying eyes.

"Mistletoe rules," he stated softly. They shared a quick smile before he slid back to his side of the seat and turned to mock-scowl at his daughter. "Happy now?"

Reese nodded with a wide grin that, thankfully, matched Heather's. "And you won't get bad luck now."

"Bad luck?" Santa asked.

"It's an old family rule—long story. But we'd better get going or none of us will make it back for the wagon rides."

"Good point." Santa took his cue and stepped on the gas, steering them toward the main zoo buildings. The no-nonsense side of Eric's consciousness went over the course of treatment for Marissa's ankle if it was only sprained, while the turned-on side registered the silky smooth texture of her skin beneath his left hand and the delicate arch of her slim foot with her sexy hot-pink toenails.

She hadn't said a word since the kiss, and he wasn't quite sure how to break the silence. For some irrational reason showing interest had been easier when he was under the impression she didn't like him. Maybe because then he automatically expected a *no* with any teasing advance he made. Now, the risk of her rejection became so much more personal with the possibility—and eager anticipation of—a *yes*.

Bold before, now he found himself sticking to a safe subject as they rolled past the African animal habitats and Christmas trees sparkling in the noon sunshine. "I really wouldn't recommend waiting until tomorrow for an X-ray."

She adjusted a fold in her tan cotton skirt. "Well, I'm not taking Heather with me, so if I can't get a hold of her father, I won't have a choice."

Eric frowned. "You don't have anyone else you can call?"

"Normally, my sister helps out, but she's gone on vacation this week." She gave a soft snort. "That's why I was late this morning. Nikki usually comes over to walk Heather to the bus stop while I'm getting ready for work."

That only served to remind him that her injury indirectly resulted from his late arrival. His jaw tightened with the reappearance of the guilt she'd sparked with her explanation about why she'd worn high heels to the zoo. It didn't matter that he wasn't the only parent to no-show, and, even if he could redo this morning, he wouldn't change his actions to avoid being late. His commanders in the Army often told him not to feel responsible for matters over which he had no control, but he'd never figured out how to shut the culpability off.

His hand flexed involuntarily on her leg. The skin beneath his fingers reminded him of the maple wood he used for his rocking chairs. Silky smooth, firm and strong, yet supple enough for him to create something special. But, like the wood, beautiful did not adequately describe the woman at his side.

There had to be some way to make up for his tardiness this morning. "My brother's home on leave this week. I can ask him or my parents to watch the girls while I drive you to the ER."

"Um…it's very kind of you to offer—"

"Here we are," Santa said, cutting off the 'but' that Eric heard in Marissa's voice. She eased her foot from his lap when the golf cart rolled to a stop.

"I couldn't help but overhear," the summer-clad Santa continued. "And if it would help, we got an X-ray machine here in the animal hospital you could use."

Eric paused in the process of getting out of the cart. "Seriously?"

"Yep."

Eric hurried around to Marissa's side to assist her down when her stubborn independence gave no indication of retreat. "That would be great," he said to Santa. "But are you sure it'll be okay?"

Santa winked at the two of them. "I ain't sleepin' with the little lady who runs this here hospital for nothin'."

Eric shared an amused yet unsure glance with Marissa. This Santa was quite the character. A short, white-haired lady bustled through the open doors of the building in front of them.

"Quit teasing them, Butch, and get over to the reindeer pens. You two, come inside and we'll have you fixed right up before he's done with the first ride."

"Aw, Judy, you always ruin my fun."

Judy glowered at him with her hands on her hips. "The children are waiting."

Santa Butch did as ordered, whistling as he drove away after a jaunty wave. Eric took advantage of Marissa's distraction and lifted her off her feet before she had a chance to protest. She clung tight to his neck in surprise while

Judy gave him an approving look on the way inside.

"You don't have to carry me everywhere," Marissa admonished.

"I'm keeping your foot elevated," Eric stated. In truth, he enjoyed the feel of her in his arms more than the brief period of elevation would help the swelling in her ankle.

Judy chuckled on her way past; Marissa rolled her eyes with a sigh. Thankfully, the sigh was accompanied by an amused twitch of the lips he'd love to kiss again.

Inside Judy's workroom, she barked out orders like the chief of surgery. No wonder Santa had rolled along with nothing more than a token protest; Eric had had drill sergeants less demanding than the elderly woman. But he had to admit, after she'd taken the X-ray, reviewed the results with him, and helped wrap Marissa's confirmed sprained ankle, Judy's efficiency would impress even the strictest general.

"Thank you," Marissa said from her perch on the table. "You have no idea how much this helped me out."

Judy patted her arm. "No problem at all,

dear. Now, I'll just call one of the merry little elves and you two will be back in the fun before you know it." She gave them a wink that mirrored Butch's from earlier. "Being *married* to Santa has its advantages."

Eric grinned at the couple's opposite ways of stating their relationship. His mother would've said, *"Typical."* Marissa's quick laugh told him she'd noted the difference, too. Then she practically hopped from the table, demonstrating the painkillers had done their job. So well in fact, she insisted on limping out to the golf cart and actually managed the journey without his help this time.

Judy hadn't been joking about the elf. Dressed in a modified summer costume not nearly as crazy as Santa's, a cute redhead a few years younger than he and Marissa sat in a cart painted with holly leaves and real candy canes strung around the top. Marissa gave the elf a smile, then paused before stepping into the vehicle. Eric followed the direction of her sweeping gaze to the bare inside rooftop.

He leaned close, his chest brushing against her back. "Disappointed?" He was—especially since he'd just caught another enticing whiff of her vanilla scent.

She cast him a glance, clearly surprised to have been caught looking for the mistletoe. Her cheeks flushed, but she gave him a good-natured chuckle and accepted the hand he offered to assist her onto the bench seat. Pleased she didn't deny it, he settled next to her with a smile and lifted her wrapped ankle to rest on his knee again. Hope glowed like a hot coal under one's breath.

Judy introduced the red headed elf as her granddaughter, Janelle, and asked her to drive them over to their group at the South Shelter. They arrived by the picnic tables at the same time Santa Butch pulled the reindeer wagon to a stop nearby. The bells draped around the reindeer's necks jingled merrily every time they shifted in their harnesses.

"How's the ankle?" Butch called.

Marissa gave him a smile and a thumbs-up. Eric was impressed at how she handled everything in stride, figuratively speaking. And through it all, her concern for her daughter eclipsed her own comfort. Even now, she showed off her Ace bandage to Heather and Reese while assuring them she'd be fine.

Patti brought them each a plate of food and they settled down at the table, only to have Santa announce the rides were beginning. Everyone else had eaten while they were at the animal hospital. Eric thought he heard a sigh from Marissa as she turned toward the wagon. She hadn't even had a chance to touch her food, and now the girls stood by her side, raring to go.

He grabbed his burger in one hand, a soda in the other, and rose to his feet before Marissa could move. "How about I ride with the girls while you put your foot up and eat your lunch?"

She hesitated, glancing from the reindeer to Heather. "Do you want me to come with you?"

"I can go with Mr. Riley," Heather said.

Marissa smiled at her daughter before looking up at Eric. "You're sure?"

"No problem. You just stay off your feet."

"You should listen to Mr. Riley, Mom. First Ponderers know all the rules."

Eric choked back a laugh at the little blond girl's stern advice.

Marissa lifted a brow at her daughter. "Oh, yeah? Says who?"

"Reese said so."

Marissa shifted her attention to Reese, whose expression reflected equal seriousness. When his daughter nodded to Marissa, Eric waited for her inevitable gem of wisdom.

"That's what Daddy says."

Good one, Reese, blame it on me. Now it was Eric's turn to receive Marissa's skeptical gaze. Somehow he kept a straight face and nodded sagely, just like his daughter. "It's true. Us Pear Medics and First Ponderers are smarter than the average Joe."

The corners of Marissa's mouth tugged upward. His gaze lingered on her shiny lips and he thought about kissing her again. Where the heck was the mistletoe when he needed it? "We do a lot of thinking," he added softly.

Her lips curved into a full smile. "Thinking is great, but how about some action?"

Eric jerked his focus back up. Laughter sparkled in the blue depths of her eyes. She lifted her chin toward the wagon behind him. "Your ride is going to leave without you."

The girls squealed and Reese grabbed his arm. "Daddy, come on!"

Eric looked over his shoulder. Indeed, Santa had climbed into the driver's seat in his red shorts and flip-flops. "All right, let's get going."

"Oh, hey, wait." Marissa dug into her bag and pulled out her camera. "Take some pictures for me."

Before he could do anything with the burger in one hand and soda in the other, she grabbed hold of his pants pocket and tugged him forward a step to slip the slim digital camera into his pocket. Reese latched onto the back waistline of his camo-pants and pulled him in the opposite direction with all her weight, making him stumble back when Marissa released her hold.

"Eric?"

While Reese continued to drag him further away, he half-turned to see Marissa smiling again.

"I like your thinking."

His heart slammed into his ribs. Oh, *hell* yeah.

"On Prancer, on Comet—"

Damn. Eric spun around at the sound of the jolly, booming voice. "Hold up there, Bu— Santa! We've got a couple more misfit toys here."

"Daddy," Reese admonished with a giggle.

Once the girls clambered aboard, Reese held his food, and Eric vaulted up beside them. The older man restarted his call to the reindeer after Eric sat on the row of hay bales behind Butch's seat.

Eric caught Marissa's gaze across the lawn. God, she was so beautiful with her blond hair framing her face. She gave a little wave when the wagon lurched forward with a merry jingling of bells, then she turned back to her food as they rode out of sight.

The girls kept him distracted, which was probably best, otherwise he'd have sat there thinking about Marissa's flirty invitation the entire time. They pointed out all the animals they'd already seen, and to his surprise, they even got most of the exotic ones right. Heather remembered the camera half way through and Eric took lots of pictures when they stopped to let each one of the kids sit on Santa's knee at

"The North Pole" near the penguin exhibit.

On their way back to the South Shelter, Patti commented how impressed she'd been with Marissa's teaching patience earlier. Eric had to agree she'd done a great job.

"I can't help but feel bad she hurt her ankle when she wasn't even supposed to be here today," the teacher said.

"You?" Eric cast her a sidelong glance. "How do you think I feel?"

Patti grimaced. "I 'spose. But at least you followed through."

"I was already on my way, I just got delayed."

"Did you get stuck behind that accident this morning? I heard about it on the bus radio. They had the highway shut down in both directions."

Eric considered the dangerous, hectic scene from that morning. *'Stuck'* was not the first word that came to his mind, but he didn't correct her. "Yeah, I was there."

"Well, see, it's not like you could've helped that," Patti rationalized.

He lifted a shoulder with a wry smile. "No more than you could've."

Heather bounded up from her hay bale perch when the wagon rolled around the corner and the shelter came back into view. She became a little too enthusiastic waving to get her mother's attention, and Eric caught her right before she tumbled off the edge. Thank goodness Marissa hadn't yet looked up from her spot against a tree.

Heather gave Eric a sheepish grin, and he couldn't help but chuckle. "You're bound and determined to keep us on our toes today, aren't you?"

"Sorry."

"Just slow down and be more careful," he gently admonished, lowering her from the wagon when it came to a stop. Reese followed the other kids and parents getting down, and Eric jumped to the ground after them. Butch stood off to the side, saying goodbye to the kids.

Eric braced a hand on each girl's shoulder, waiting until the crowd thinned. "Thank Santa for the ride."

Reese and Heather sounded a chorus of thanks before taking off across the asphalt path toward Marissa. Eric made sure they reached the tree before turning around to face the older man.

"This was great. Thanks."

"You're welcome." Butch shifted his gaze toward Marissa and the girls. "So, I expect you'll be taking the lady and her daughter home?"

"Ah..." Eric frowned, wondering where the man would get that idea.

Butch backhanded him on the arm. "Open your eyes, boy. She can't drive with her foot all wrapped up like that."

Eric absently flexed his shoulder as Butch climbed back up to the driver's bench. The old guy might be...*old*, but he still packed a wallop. Then his words registered. Eric's gaze went straight to where Marissa sat, smiling up at the girls, her foot extended in front of her. He started to smile, too, unconsciously straightening.

Santa was absolutely right.

Butch gave a merry chuckle. "Got ya thinking, now, don't I?"

Eric reached up to clasp the man's hand with

a grin of appreciation. He'd been dreading the end of the field trip without even realizing it. Now he didn't have to figure out a clever way to see her again to collect on the invitation from earlier. When he started to back away from the wagon, Butch tossed a handful of leaves down toward him. Eric caught them, then laughed.

Mistletoe. Santa was handing out presents early this year. Eric eased the green sprig into one of his pockets, careful not to crush the precious gift.

Santa Butch winked at him before lifting the reins to urge the reindeer forward. Over his shoulder he called, "Merry Christmas to all, and to all a good night!"

Chapter 5

To avoid staring across the lawn at Eric, Marissa concentrated on the girls. He was the ultimate picture of a man, standing there talking with Santa Butch. Dark hair, amazing gray eyes, sexy voice, a killer body, and a good dad. What was not to like?

And yet, she still couldn't believe her own provocative words earlier. *I like your thinking.*

Sure, he'd been staring at her still-tingling mouth, but it didn't mean he fantasized about a repeat of the mistletoe kiss like she had been. A much more *private* repeat—especially now that she knew he wasn't married.

But to pretty much outright invite another kiss? She didn't do things like that anymore.

Just the thought of getting involved with a man again made her heart beat faster. She'd managed not to think about it much over the past few years—kept too busy on purpose. It had been a long time, and heaven help her, as attracted as she was to Eric, it scared the daylights out of her.

Good, God, live a little! No wonder you haven't had a date in three years.

"Your dad is fun."

Heather's words registered on Marissa's conscious just as Reese replied, "I know. I wish I could stay with Daddy all the time."

Marissa tore her gaze away from Eric at the dark haired little girl's plaintive words. The two had moved away a few feet and were talking to each other in their own little world.

"I live with my mom 'cause my dad's always busy," Heather said matter-of-factly. "He never bothers with stuff like this."

"Daddy works a lot, too. Mom says he doesn't have time for me and that's why he only comes to see me every other weekend."

Marissa's heart ached for both little girls who so obviously needed their fathers. She usually made excuses for Ted to Heather to spare her daughter's feelings and protect her. Judging by Heather's choice of words, Marissa hadn't succeeded—or maybe it was that Ted hadn't fooled her? Either way, she didn't like it.

The fear she'd tried to squash moments ago breathed new life. Things were so different from her college years when she'd dated and had fun. There was so much more at risk now than just her heart.

Her gaze strayed to Eric, who backed toward them, still in conversation with Santa Butch. He appeared the perfect dad today. Except from the sound of Reese's words, it was nothing but an act to look good in front of everyone. Hadn't she seen the evidence when he couldn't be counted on to show up on time to fulfill his responsibilities? When he didn't even bother to apologize to his daughter or the people he'd inconvenienced?

Considering her past experience, she should've seen it coming instead of being blinded by physical reactions. A picture of Ted flashed in her mind. These damn men had no clue what they were doing to their kids. Or if they did, they sure as hell didn't seem to care.

Across the grass, the school bus pulled into the parking lot. A quick glance at her watch confirmed it was time to go home. A weak wave of relief gave way under an overpowering swell of unwelcome disappointment.

Exasperated at the second emotion, Marissa yanked her bag from under her calf. She grimaced when her foot hit the dirt, but the jolt of pain to her ankle mirrored the reality check she'd just received.

Yes, Eric Riley was sinfully good-looking, and yes, thank God he'd saved her daughter on the giraffe platform, but even that only served to point out the danger in losing her focus on what was important—*Heather*.

Slinging the handles of her bag over her shoulder, she pushed up off the ground. Thanks to inconsiderate people, she still had a lot of work to do tonight and—

"Let me give you a hand."

Eric's deep voice reached her ears just before his boots and camouflaged pants entered her peripheral vision. She had no time to protest as one large hand grasped her elbow, another slid along her waist; both lifted. Sensation rocketed through her at his mere touch. Awareness heightened when she stood beside him, her shoulder against his chest. He'd released her arm, but the warm hand on her waist slipped low to rest on her hip.

The elusive pine scent from earlier teased her nostrils. Him, her imagination, or the tree they stood beneath? She inhaled discreetly. Clean, fresh pine unspoiled by underlying chemicals of cologne left her unable to confirm the origin of the fragrance. The only way to be sure would be to bury her nose against his skin. Her gaze zeroed in on the tan column of his neck, and she swayed slightly.

"Mom, do we have to go home now?"

Eric's hand steadied her. Marissa jerked her head toward her daughter.

"You good?" Eric asked in a low tone close to her ear.

His warm breath stirred her hair, sending a shiver down her back. When she realized he'd asked if she had her balance on her uninjured foot, Marissa nodded, not trusting her voice for fear it would betray her like the rest of her body. The fingers on her hip flexed briefly before they fell away. She missed his touch almost immediately.

She clenched her jaw in frustration. How ridiculous. He was just a man. So what if he was sexy as hell, she'd decided years ago never to depend on the male species again. Especially one who wasn't there for his kid.

She limped a step away from Eric and turned to Heather. "Yes, honey, it's time to go home."

"Aw, mom, I want to play with Reese yet."

"You'll see Reese at school on Monday," Marissa said.

The summer school teacher detoured in their direction on the way to the bus with her group of kids. "Eric, is it safe to assume Reese will be riding home with you?" Patti asked.

He put his hands on Reese's shoulders. "She will. Thanks for checking."

Patti turned to Marissa, her expression contrite. "I can't thank you enough for your help today, though I'm very sorry about your ankle."

"It's not your fault. And I'll be fine, don't worry about me," Marissa assured her. "I had a great time with the girls today."

Not to mention one heck of a kiss under the mistletoe, a small voice in her head reminded.

Patti smiled, her glance swinging toward the idling bus. "Ultimately, that is what matters most. We'd better get going before they leave without us. See you on Monday."

"Bye." After the teacher left, Marissa took a deep breath to face Eric. Time to say goodbye to him too, before she went completely insane and forgot she'd changed her mind about him. The moment she met his smiling, smoky gray gaze, her pulse jerked. Too bad her body hadn't gotten the memo from her brain yet. "Maybe we'll see you at school sometime."

Bewilderment clouded his eyes at her intentionally casual statement. And no wonder after the way she'd flirted before the reindeer wagon rides. Embarrassment warmed her cheeks with the remembrance.

"Actually," he said, "I'm thinking you two need a ride home."

Heather clapped in excitement. "Please, Mom, please?" she begged. "Can we ride home with them?"

"Please, Mrs. Wilder?" Reese added.

Marissa resisted their enthusiasm; somewhat annoyed he'd make the suggestion in front of the girls. She forced a polite smile to her lips and said pointedly to Eric, "I have my car here, remember?"

"You can't drive with a sprained ankle," he countered. When she opened her mouth to argue, he quietly added, "It wouldn't be safe for Heather."

She shut her mouth and stared toward the parking lot. He was right. She might not be able to slam on the brakes if something unexpected happened, not to mention accelerating wouldn't be too fun, either. How had he known to bring up Heather's safety before anything else?

Any good parent thinks of their child first.

Maybe she should give him the benefit of the doubt...

Marissa stomped on that thought. Damn it, *no*. She wasn't going to overlook the fact that his daughter needed him more than he made himself available. Just because she made excuses for Ted's irresponsibility to spare her daughter's feelings didn't mean she accepted him constantly letting their little girl down. It was no different with Eric.

"How am I supposed to get my car home?" she argued half-heartedly, knowing they'd be riding home with him and Reese no matter what.

"I'll get a ride back here tomorrow to get yours and then I can drop it by your house."

It made perfect sense, but, gol-darn it, why'd he have to be so nice about it when she'd rather argue?

"It's the least I can do after messing up your whole day."

See? His consideration joined forces with her physical attraction, chipping away at her defensive indignation for his daughter. It didn't help that both girls waited expectantly, Heather's expression reminiscent of the one she wore every Christmas morning.

"Since it sounds like everything's settled, I guess we should get going," Marissa said.

Heather and Reese let out whoops of joy and raced toward the parking lot.

"Slow down," Eric called. "Wait by the edge of the grass."

Marissa tried to ignore her unwelcome anticipation and limped after them.

"Is everything okay?" Eric asked from beside her. "You seem upset for some reason."

She kept her gaze focused on the ground. "I'm just a little tired."

Coward. If she were smart, she'd tell him exactly what she thought of him and get rid of any attraction once and for all.

"I'd be happy to carry you," Eric offered, his tone a little deeper than before, even though she could hear a grin in his voice.

Her stomach did a somersault and she quickly snapped, "I'm fine."

He didn't speak the rest of the way to his truck, his confusion tangible in the silence. She did her best not to feel guilty, because, really, *she* had nothing to feel bad about. After lifting the girls into the back of his extended cab and making sure they were buckled tight, he stepped out of the way so she could climb up, but didn't offer assistance. Marissa told herself that was fine with her. He closed her door and walked around the front to settle in the driver's seat.

"Where we headed?" He started the truck to

reverse from the parking spot.

Marissa gave him their address a couple miles northeast of Pulaski, the girls' whispers and giggles in the back seat their background music.

"That's only a couple miles from my house." Eric navigated onto the state highway. "If you don't mind stopping, I'm almost positive I have a pair of crutches in my basement from when my sister broke her leg a few years ago. You might want to use them until you can see your doctor on Monday."

Much as she wanted to get home, crutches would definitely help, so she nodded. Fifteen minutes later, when they turned onto an older residential street, Reese's head popped up between the seats. "We're going to our house? Cool! Can I show Heather my room?"

Eric glanced up into the rearview mirror. "Sit back in your seat, Reese. We're only stopping for a minute. Mrs. Wilder is tired."

"Aww, man," both girls chorused with disappointment.

Marissa loved how he put it on her. Earlier he'd been the fun one and now she ruined everything because she was tired. Biting back a sigh of annoyance, she resigned herself to a little longer enduring her conflicting emotions in his presence. "I guess we could stay for a couple minutes."

The moment he turned into his driveway, a beautifully carved sign next to his mailbox caught her attention. *Riley Custom Creations*. When they rounded a corner of the drive, all it took was one look at the log house set back on the wooded lot, and she wanted her own tour.

"Wow, this is beautiful."

"Daddy and Uncle Mark built it," Reese announced.

Marissa raised her brows. "Really?"

"It's a work in progress," Eric said.

"Daddy also makes tables and chairs and stuff," Reese added.

Eric hit the button on the visor for the automatic garage opener, but parked outside while the stall door in front of them rose. After he opened the truck door, Reese climbed out so fast he barely got out of his seat.

"Come on, Heather, let's go!"

Marissa couldn't help a smile at their

excitement. It was hard to believe the two had only met at summer school three weeks ago, thanks to a realignment of the school district boundaries.

"Those two are like miniature tornados," Eric muttered with a grin when they'd disappeared inside. In direct contrast to his lack of assistance getting her into the truck, now he hurried around to her side and grasped her elbow to steady her on the climb down. Awareness raced along her limbs. Her skin tingled from the warmth of his touch.

"Come put your foot up in the living room while go I dig those crutches out of the downstairs closet."

He slowly led her through the garage and kitchen, to an open-concept living room with huge picture windows on one side, and a railed loft above. Giggles and thumps could be heard up an iron and half log staircase to the right of the loft, revealing the location of Reese's room.

Marissa stared at the gently spiraling staircase in amazement. Completely unexpected in a log home, somehow it looked just right.

"Make yourself at home." Eric pointed to a

dark brown couch. "I'll be back in a minute."

He disappeared down a second set of spiral stairs, which must lead to a basement. Curiosity brought her to one of the windows instead of the couch. It appeared the basement was a walkout because to her right there was a large, split-level porch off the kitchen, with steps leading down to a patio directly below where she stood. A swing set and play area for Reese sat on one side of the expansive backyard, and another log structure dominated the other side. A sign identical to the one by the mailbox hung above a set of double doors, identifying the structure as Eric's workshop.

His grass needed mowing, and a pile of sawdust and leftover wood pieces covered the workshop porch, but otherwise the backyard looked like a picture out of a country homes magazine. She pivoted slowly to take in the carpeted living room, loving the knotty pine walls and a fieldstone fireplace. Her glimpse of the kitchen left her equally impressed by its bright, spacious dining area, a gorgeous hunter green tile countertop and stunning cabinets that glowed rich amber beneath their varnish.

She'd love to go into his kitchen to explore, but her ankle had begun to throb again, so she made her way to the couch and sat down. Her gaze continued to take in the nuances of the space around her, and she realized with surprise that beyond the actual house itself, he hadn't done much with the place. Yet, because of the beauty of the wood, the bare walls and tabletops were not immediately noticeable.

The empty end table between the couch and a worn chair caught her attention. Made of a square of wood and four black iron legs, it was a simple design, but after one look at the top, she knew she wouldn't want to put anything on it, either. Fall colored leaves of red, orange and yellow spilled across the unstained pine wood that was covered with coats of varnish until no leaf tip or stem marred the surface. She ran her fingers across it, enjoying the cool, silky smoothness beneath her touch.

Footsteps sounded on the stairs a moment before Eric reappeared from the basement with the crutches in hand.

"Is this one of yours?" Marissa asked, still caressing the table.

"That is Reese's accidental creation," he said, standing next to the couch by her. "I had other plans for the top, but last fall she brought in an armful of leaves as I was working and dropped them on the table so she could show me her favorite one." He pointed to a brilliant red maple leaf. "We finished the table together, and she decided it needed to be right here so I'd think about her when she's at her mother's."

His expression told her he cherished the memory and she thought about how Ted never did anything like that with Heather. More conflicting evidence to shake her weakening resolve not to get involved with Eric. The heart of the problem was that her past-biased inner arguments didn't stack up against the proof in front of her face.

"It's a great piece," Marissa said past the sudden lump in her throat.

"Thanks. We think so, too." Eric lifted a crutch. "You want to give these a try?"

Marissa stood up and fit them under arms, but they were a little too high until Eric adjusted them. After taking a turn around the living room, she gave him a reluctant yet grateful smile. "These really help, thanks."

"No problem."

"Hi, Mom."

She looked up to see Heather and Reese grinning over the loft railing at them. "Hey. Come on down now, we need to get going."

"Aw, Mommm. Can't we stay longer?"

Marissa shook her head. "Sorry, honey—"

"You really should stay off your feet for tonight," Eric interrupted. "Why don't you stay, and I'll order dinner for all of us."

Her gratitude for the crutches vanished when both girls raced down the stairs in full-throttle begging mode. He'd done it again, asking in front of them so if she refused she'd be the bad guy. She forced another smile to cover her annoyance, but kept her tone firm. "I'm sure you have plans, we don't want to intrude."

"Our plans consist of calling Figaro's Pizza and roasting marshmallows for s'mores after dinner."

Over the heads of the still-pleading girls, she glared at him for not taking her obvious hint. He met her gaze, then crossed his arms over his chest. Unlike earlier when he seemed confused about her reserved demeanor, now he just appeared defiant. A determined glint in his eyes sent her heart hammering against her ribs in anticipation.

Good Lord, it isn't fair. She broke eye contact in an effort to maintain her waffling resentment.

Heather tugged on her arm. "Come on, Mom, you *love* Figaro's."

She didn't even have to look up to see Eric's smug grin at that statement.

"Daddy says I make the best s'mores—I'll make you one," Reese added.

She looked from one precious face to the other, knowing she'd lost but not sure how to concede gracefully. And without Eric thinking he'd won, the slimy snake. Unfortunately, her mind seemed to have jumped on the bandwagon with her body, because she couldn't think of a single sentence that would put him in his place and accept his invitation to dinner at the same time.

She concentrated on Reese. "Do you burn the marshmallows, or toast them golden brown?"

"I toast them," she answered. "Daddy always

burns his, that's why he says mine are better."

"Then as long as *you* make my s'mores, we'll stay."

"All right!" Heather threw her arms around Marissa's waist, making her hop back a step to keep their balance. "Thanks, Mom."

Marissa hugged her daughter back and finally allowed a quick glance at Eric. He smiled, but surprisingly, no triumph gleamed in his expression. He dropped his gaze to his daughter.

"Reese, I had a surprise for later, but since Heather is here, I might as well tell you now…I finished the treehouse this week."

Reese's eyes rounded and a grin split her face. She launched herself into her father's arms. "You're the best!"

"Why don't you two go check it out?"

Reese wriggled free of Eric's hold. Heather wasted no time running after her through the French doors in the kitchen and down the porch stairs to the patio. Marissa maneuvered to the window with the crutches and watched them cross the yard to a tree in the back.

Once they were up the ladder of the tree

house, and she was sure they would be occupied for a good long time, she rounded on Eric with her heart pounding.

"You've got some nerve."

Chapter 6

*M*arissa's verbal attack sent Eric's eyebrows skyward. She wore a fierce scowl, her body as rigid as a piece of lumber in his shop. He decided it was high time he figured out what the hell was going on.

"For what?" He shoved his hands into his pockets to hide his clenched fingers. "Kissing you under the mistletoe, or offering dinner?"

Her cheeks flushed crimson. From anger, or did she remember their kiss with the same sensual clarity as he did?

"For making me the Wicked Witch."

Anger. The desire to stride over and haul her against him battled his control. "When did I do that?"

"When you brought up the ride home, coming inside, and staying for dinner, always in front of the girls, where *I'd* look like the bad guy if I said no."

Ah…yeah, she did have a point, but in his defense, only the last time had been intentional. "What do you expect?" he asked, fingering the crushed mistletoe leaves in his pocket. "With all the conflicting signals you've been giving out today, I had to use any ammunition I could find."

"Oh, please." Yet she avoided his gaze by limping toward the kitchen. "Only a jerk uses kids for his own personal gain."

"And what the hell would I have to gain from this?" He gave a disbelieving laugh as he followed her. "You're the one who switched gears the moment we got back from the reindeer rides. I'd just like to know what happened."

"So it's my fault?" She shook her head. "How typical."

He released a frustrated breath and took hold of her arm, turning her to face him. "I'm not blaming you, Marissa, but how do you explain *see you around* right after *I like what you're thinking*? And don't even try to tell me you didn't know exactly what was on my mind."

His gaze lowered. Even now, the lure of her lips, the desire to really, truly taste her, was hard to resist.

She shrugged his hand away and took a deep breath. "Maybe I'm just not interested anymore, did *that* cross your mind?"

"Maybe? Anymore?" He dipped his chin to get a better look at her face, but she frowned and turned her back to him. He relaxed a little with her silent answer and leaned in close against her back to speak next to her ear. "Now we're getting somewhere."

She ducked her head to the side, tossing him an annoyed glance over her shoulder. "No, we're not, and I'm sure the girls would like dinner sometime tonight."

"Marissa. If you want me to leave you alone, all you have to do is say so."

She drew in a breath as if prepared with a reply, but then…nothing. After a few seconds of silence, she suddenly straightened her shoulders. "Yes, of course that's what I want. I want you to leave me alone."

He chuckled. "Who are you trying to convince, me or you?"

She turned around. "What?"

"Look me in the eye and tell me you don't like me."

She gave a short laugh, her gaze fixed on his chest. "Wow, I should've known with your looks you'd turn out to be arrogant."

A loud snort accompanied the slide of the screen door behind him. "Eric is arrogant in spite of his looks, not because of them."

Eric spun around at the sound of his brother's voice. He flashed him a look. *Impeccable timing as always, bro.* Mark lifted his shoulder with a smart-ass grin and walked up to Marissa with his hand extended.

"Mark Riley. And he can't be arrogant about his looks because *I'm* the good-looking one."

She shook his hand, and Eric swore her laugh held a note of relief.

"Marissa Wilder. It runs in the family, doesn't it?"

Mark's smile widened. "Yes, thank you."

"I meant the arrogance."

Mark clutched his chest with his right hand.

"Ooh, ouch."

Eric chuckled then, enjoying her quick-witted sparring with his brother, and the fact that she thought he was good-looking. *Him*, not his brother. He raised an eyebrow at Mark, wondering how much he'd heard through the screen. "So, what's up?"

"Nothing much. I saw the truck and figured I'd stop by to see my niece. I didn't know you had company."

"Reese is in the treehouse with Marissa's daughter, Heather."

Mark leaned back to look outside. "I thought I heard voices out there."

"Only our conversation sounded more interesting, right?" Eric asked.

"Hell yeah," Mark agreed without apology. He rubbed his hands together in anticipation, leaned against the counter and crossed his arms over his chest. "Please, continue."

Marissa fit the crutches under her arms and shook her head. "Sorry, that conversation is definitely over. Besides, my ankle is starting to hurt again, and I'd love something to drink."

Mark's backhand caught Eric on the same

shoulder where Butch had smacked him. "You didn't offer the lady a beverage?" Before Eric could mount a defense, Mark shook his head in apology at Marissa. "Younger brothers, I tell you. What can I get for you?"

"That depends on what he's got."

Mark opened Eric's refrigerator. Eric crossed his arms over his chest and mimicked his brother's earlier pose as Mark proceeded to give Marissa a list of options including water, beer, soda, milk, wine or Kool-Aid. She chose red wine and the two of them critiqued the quality of his bottle from the Chianti Classico region of Italy.

Eric glared at his brother's back; Mark didn't know shit about wine. Jealousy stirred in his gut despite the fact that he knew his brother was purposely trying to rile him.

Mark steered Marissa toward the door leading to the porch before turning back to pour a glass of wine. "You relax out there and elevate your foot while I teach Eric some manners."

She gave Eric a sassy grin and limped past with the crutches. Mark pushed the full glass into his hand. "Lesson one: never keep a woman waiting."

"Paybacks are a bitch," Eric warned in a low tone before striding over in time to slide open the screen door for Marissa.

"What's for dinner?" Mark asked.

"Not sure what you're having, but we're ordering pizza." Eric set the glass of wine on the patio table before pulling over another chair and arranging the cushions for Marissa to prop her foot on.

"Great," Mark said from inside. "That leads right into lesson number two: no onions."

Eric hung his head in defeat. Marissa covered her mouth, but he still heard her laugh and couldn't help a smile of his own. Despite Mark's obnoxious act, Marissa seemed to have relaxed some, so maybe he wouldn't kick his brother's ass just yet.

"Hey, by the way," Mark called, his voice muffled by the refrigerator door. "I ran into Charlie in Redemption this afternoon."

The mention of fellow EMT Charlie Russell made Eric straighten quick and head back inside.

"Your guy from that accident this morning has been upgraded from critical to serious. He's still in intensive care, but things look good," Mark continued.

"That's great news. Listen, I wanted to—"

"Are you talking about the accident on the highway earlier?" Marissa asked before Eric could change the subject. "It was all over the radio this morning—I had to take a detour to the zoo."

"Yep." Mark clapped Eric on the shoulder. "The driver of the SUV probably wouldn't have made it if Eric hadn't been there."

Much as he was glad to hear the man would recover, he wasn't comfortable getting into details in front of Marissa. Eric grabbed a glass and the bottle of wine to pour a drink, giving Mark a slight frown to discourage further elaboration. "We do what we need to, you know that as well as anyone."

"Yeah, but I also know we don't always hear how they're doing." Mark took a swig of the soda he'd swiped from the fridge.

"Mark's a medic in the army just like I was, only he lasted longer than I did." Eric explained to Marissa, hoping to detour the conversation.

"How long is that?" she asked.

"Fifteen years next month. I'm home for my last week of leave before I get out in December."

"What are you going to do then?"

"I've been thinking about investing in a business or something around here. Maybe look into opening a small resort."

"I didn't know about this," Eric said as Mark stepped out onto the porch by Marissa.

"I've been toying with the idea for a little while."

"What kind of resort?" Marissa asked.

"Something with cabins, near a lake so there'd be swimming and water-skiing in the summer, and snowmobiling and ice-fishing in the winter."

"Anything near water is going to cost a pretty penny," Eric commented as he stepped outside and slid the screen shut again.

"I haven't spent much in the military, so I've got a bit saved. Plus, after helping you with this place, I figure I'll get some free labor down the road, right?"

"You can count on it," Eric said.

Mark pulled out a chair as if he planned to join them for the evening. Normally Eric would relish the chance to visit with his older brother, but right now he was feeling somewhat territorial over Marissa. He hadn't met anyone that interested him like she did since his divorce, so the way he saw it, his selfishness was justified.

Just as he was trying to come up with a nice way to tell his brother to bug off, Mark looked over and caught his eye. With a knowing grin, he indicated Eric should take the seat.

"I'm going to get going, but you've got Reese all weekend, right?"

Still standing, Eric nodded. "I talked Nina into a couple extra days. I'm guessing the pregnancy has her pretty tired, because it didn't become the war I expected."

"Good, then I'll let Reese play with her friend and stop by tomorrow."

"Speaking of tomorrow, would you have some time to give me a ride back to the zoo to pick up Marissa's car?"

"Sure." Mark winked at Marissa. "Anything

for a pretty woman."

She shook her head. "Even a blind person could tell you two are brothers."

"Taught him everything he knows," Mark boasted.

"Oh, God," Eric groaned. "How about we just see you tomorrow—please?"

Mark took hold of Marissa's hand. "Keep this guy in line."

"I'll try. Nice to meet you, Mark."

"Sweetheart, the pleasure is all mine." He bent and lifted her hand to his lips.

Eric gave him a shove on the shoulder, only half-joking. "Get the hell outta here."

Mark laughed on his way down the steps, waved when Reese hollered, "Hi, Uncle Mark!" but continued to his Jeep parked near Eric's workshop. A couple honks of the horn and he was gone.

Eric turned to Marissa with a wry smile. "I am very sorry for all of that."

"Don't worry about it. He was funny, and he seems like a nice guy."

"*Seems* being the operative word." He glanced at his watch. "I better get dinner ordered—what do you and Heather like on your pizza?"

She gave him their preferences and though it was stupid, Eric grinned when she didn't ask for onions. It could be she just didn't like the breath-destroying vegetable, but he preferred to look at it as a continuation of her 'maybe' from earlier. Hell, she'd totally avoided answering when he'd told her to say she didn't like him to his face. That had to mean something right?

Hopefully the mistletoe would still be recognizable if—*when*—he got the chance to use it. No way he was letting that gift go to waste.

"They'll be here in about twenty-five minutes," he called after he hung up the phone. "Can I top off your glass?"

"Not until dinner, but thanks. So, any other brothers that might pop in?" she asked as he came out to take a seat kitty-corner from her at the patio table.

"No, he's one of a kind. I've got a younger sister in Ohio and though my parents only live about ten minutes from here, they usually call first."

Eric himself had never lived farther than a fifteen-mile radius from where he was born except for his six years in the Army. He supposed he should be grateful Nina left him for another Pulaski native. While the drama had set the town gossips' tongues on fire, at least Reese remained close. He shook off those thoughts and returned his attention to Marissa.

"How about you? Brothers? Sisters?"

"One younger sister, Nikki. She lives a couple blocks away from me."

He gave her a thoughtful look as he searched his memory. "You didn't grow up here, did you? I don't think you're that much younger than me, and Pulaski is not so big that I wouldn't remember."

She raised her eyebrows. "And you are how old?"

"Twenty-nine." He paused, but went for it anyway. "Dare I ask the same?"

"I'm twenty-seven," she said with a smile. "And I grew up in Milwaukee, that's why you don't remember me."

"A big city girl. What brought you to our small town?"

"Oh, God, it's such a cliché."

Her laugh was slightly embarrassed and he guessed, "You followed a guy."

"Yeah." She dropped her gaze and tilted her wine glass, studying the liquid inside. "My college sweetheart, who turned out to be sweet on every girl but me shortly after Heather was born."

"He's an idiot."

That statement got him another brief smile.

"I'd already fallen in love with the town, so I didn't mind staying after the divorce," she continued. "My sister had just graduated high school and couldn't wait to get out of the house, so she moved in with me and helped out while going to college. She bought her own place a couple months ago."

"It's nice to have family nearby."

"It is," she agreed. "Especially since my ex isn't very involved."

His was too involved, but for all the wrong reasons. Eric finished off his glass and switched back to a previous subject. "I still can't believe we live so close and haven't met. Especially with the kids at the same school."

"But they weren't until a couple weeks ago. Heather used to go to Hillcrest but when they rezoned the school districts, we were shifted to Lannoye. I signed her up for a couple summer school classes so she could hopefully make a few friends before the regular school year starts."

"Okay, that makes much more sense." Laughter and and the sound of footsteps clambering down the tree house steps drew Eric's attention. "And it worked—those two are quickly becoming inseparable."

Marissa smiled as the girls ran across the yard toward them.

"Dad—pizza's here!"

After dinner, the girls cleared the patio table while Eric and Marissa finished their second glasses of wine. Eric marveled at how well the evening turned out after the shaky middle to their day. He wasn't sure if the catalyst had been their argument, or somehow resulted from Mark's annoying antics, but he'd take the camaraderie and easy conversation however he could get it.

The girls had gone inside and he heard the dishwasher door open. The clink of silverware and and clatter of plates accompanied Reese's voice through the screen door. "I always help Daddy 'cuz he has no one to take care of him when I'm not here."

Chin resting in the palm of her hand, Marissa cast Eric a glance and a smile. "Impressive."

He leaned closer and whispered, "I redo most of what she does after she goes to bed, but I'll never tell her that."

"Gosh, no, you have to take what you can get."

Funny, her words mirrored his thoughts almost exactly.

"It's always me and Mom, my dad's never around," Eric heard Heather say. "You're lucky your dad is cool."

"So's your mom," Reese said. "My mom is okay sometimes, but I really wish I could stay here with Daddy more."

A painful lump formed in Eric's throat. He swirled the last little bit of wine in his glass, hoping with all his heart he could grant that wish very soon. Marissa remained silent after that comment and suddenly Reese and Heather were at the screen door.

"Daddy, the kitchen's clean, can we start the campfire now?"

In typical six-year old fashion, they switched gears in the blink of an eye. He caught Marissa's gaze. "Your ankle good enough for a quick tour?"

She sat up straighter, a look of anticipation warming his heart. "Yes, definitely. I've been wanting to see the rest of the house."

Eric faced the girls when they came out onto the porch. "Give me a few minutes to show Marissa around, then we'll get the fire going, okay?"

"Okay. We'll be in the treehouse." Reese grabbed Heather's arm to pull her along, down the stairs. "Don't forget to call us."

"We won't," Eric promised.

He took Marissa through the house first. It was gratifying to see everything through her eyes and hear her admiration for the work he and Mark had done. A walk through the basement revealed what he had to do yet, and then he led her out to his workshop.

"Sorry for the mess—give me a minute to sweep up."

She stopped him when he reached for a broom. "I don't mind, leave it. I love the smell of fresh cut pine."

Propping the crutches by the door, she limped barefoot across the floor. She dragged a rocking chair he'd crafted out of maple away from the side wall and sat down. The chair rocked gently from a push of her uninjured foot. Delicate fingers caressed the flawlessly sanded wood. Her quietly voiced appreciation of the quality of his creation made his chest expand.

It took a moment to realize the sudden swell of emotion wasn't a simple matter of pride in a good piece of work created from his own hands, it was *her*.

He hadn't been looking for anyone special in his life right now past Reese. Yet after only one day with Marissa and her daughter, he could picture himself and the beautiful blond in front of him tucking the girls into bed together before cuddling on the couch to watch a movie. Or better yet, making love in his king size bed with the firelight flickering across her golden skin.

Then they'd sleep in the next morning until the girls woke them up for breakfast.

It was totally crazy to think of a future with this woman and her daughter already, but think of it he did. His heart rate picked up, and he turned to brace his hands on the windowsill until he'd taken a couple of deep breaths. He'd have to be careful not to rush any attempt to get past her defenses and risk chasing her away.

"Eric?"

He turned around at Marissa's soft, hesitant voice.

"Um..." She ran her palms up and down the smooth arms of the rocking chair. "I owe you an apology."

"For what?"

"This morning...and then later, after the reindeer rides." She met his gaze, her eyes full of remorse; the height of her cheekbones colored a pretty shade of pink. "First of all, I assumed you'd forgotten the field trip, and I was angry for Reese's sake because it was something my ex would've done. I know how disappointed Heather is whenever Ted says he'll be there and then never shows."

Eric absorbed that, but wasn't sure how to respond. Being compared to a man that even a six-year old didn't seem to respect was a bit of a reality check after what he'd just been thinking. He didn't like the feeling one bit.

A slight frown creased her brow. "Why didn't you tell us you were at the accident this morning? I mean, you saved a man's life."

Eric leaned back against the windowsill. "It's not something I brag about, I just do what has to be done. It's part of the job."

"Explaining why you were late is not bragging," she rationalized.

He lifted a shoulder, unwilling to discuss the subject further.

"Okay, then...continuing on with my humiliation..." She gave him a sheepish smile. "After judging you completely irresponsible, I then jumped to the conclusion you were hitting on me while you were married."

He held up his bare left hand.

"Yeah, I know, but Ted never wore his ring, either."

Eric crossed his arms over his chest with a scowl. "I'm not so sure I like the theme of this conversation."

"Let me finish or I won't get it all out."

"There's more?"

She cringed and nodded at the same time. "The thing is, my ex has joint custody of Heather, only he doesn't bother to show up but maybe four or five times a year. I've tried to protect Heather, I've made countless excuses for him, but as you heard earlier, Heather's got him all figured out anyway."

Eric growled. "Added to what you said earlier, he sounds like a selfish jackass."

"Yeah, pretty much." She paused, and he saw her struggle to form her words. Her reluctant gaze met his. "Based on that experience, a couple of, um, innocent comments Reese made this afternoon led me to believe that you weren't available to her when she needed you, either."

His remorse over the past rushed forward with dizzying speed. He dropped his arms to his side while straightening from the window. "What'd she say?"

Marissa sat forward in the chair, her hands clasped in her lap. "You have to understand that it was because of my wrong assumptions that they sounded bad."

"What'd she say?"

She sighed again. "Just that she wished she could see you more, and that her mom said you didn't have time for her."

Eric's hand clenched at his side. "Unfortunately, there was a time Nina would've been justified in saying that—to *me*, not our daughter. This past year I've done whatever I can to make sure Reese knows she's the single most important person in my life, but Nina still looks for any reason to cut me down in front of her."

He paused for a breath only to have the meaning of Marissa's earlier words finally hit home. Heat rushed through his body as he captured her gaze with his. "So let me get this straight—you've been comparing me to your ex *all* day?"

The guilt in her expression said it all.

"Wow." He ran a hand through his hair, grasped the back of his neck for a moment, then dropped his arm in defeat. "I made a hell of a first impression on you, didn't I?"

She pushed to her feet and took a step forward, her hand outstretched. "No, Eric, it's not you, it's me—"

"Breaking up with me already?" he exclaimed with light sarcasm. "We haven't even had our first date yet."

And the way things were going, they weren't likely to, either.

She limped closer. "Honestly? It's because of my initial reactions to you this morning that I went the wrong direction. I've focused all my attention on Heather since my divorce five years ago, so basically, when you add in my marriage, I haven't dated for almost eight years."

He'd only had a couple dates after Nina left him more than a year ago, but he'd rather hear her story.

"After Ted, I haven't even been attracted to anyone until...um, until today." She met his eyes, that cute pink tinge spreading across her cheeks again. "You really threw me off balance. In self-defense, I exaggerated reasons *not* to like you so I wouldn't think so much about wanting to...kiss you again." Her blush deepened. "But you kept being so nice, and—"

"Charming?" he interjected. A grin emerged, full of rekindled hope.

"Don't push it," she warned, only she ruined it with a smile of her own. "*And*, tonight I saw the way you were with not only Reese, but Heather as well, and I realized I'd projected all my insecurities about my past onto you, which isn't fair at all. Because I shouldn't automatically assume you'll cheat on me, or ignore the girls when you decide you have something better to do—or what about later, if we…um…"

Her lashes quickly lowered. She visibly swallowed the rest of her words while her face flared bright red.

"If we…?" he prompted, curious to see how far into the future *her* thoughts had traveled.

Marissa shook her head. "Nothing, forget it."

"Not so fast," Eric protested when she hobbled toward the workshop door.

She paused near the opening, but didn't face him. "Listen, I know we only just met, so assuming we'd have any type of relationship—especially now—well, that's just a little crazy and..." Her hands flailed in the silence, as if their movement would locate the words she sought. "I'm sorry—for everything. And I should've just apologized and then shut up. I will shut up right now. In fact, it's probably time to go—"

Eric grasped her shoulders from behind, stalling her departure. She jumped about an inch. He hunched his own shoulders and pressed his cheek next to her ear. "You're doing it again."

"What?"

"Assuming the wrong things when we're actually on the same page."

Her breath caught. "We are?"

"I've been planning to ask you to dinner ever since I noticed you weren't wearing a ring." He turned her around and locked his gaze with her beautiful blue eyes. With one hand, he trailed his knuckles softly along her cheek before tucking her long hair back over her shoulder. "Not to mention, imagining our second kiss without an audience has been driving me crazy."

Chapter 7

*M*arissa wouldn't have thought it possible, but his low-voiced statement made her pulse race even faster. He was going to kiss her again. She wanted his mouth on hers more than she'd wanted anything in a very long time.

A sudden attack of nervousness made her glance out the window in the gathering darkness toward the back of the yard where the girls still played. Beams of light filtered through the thick foliage concealing the tree house windows.

"They're fine," Eric assured her, mistakenly guessing the reason for her hesitation. She didn't correct him. He threaded his calloused fingers through the hair at the nape of her neck.

Tingles radiated down her spine from his warm touch.

Marissa cleared her throat and met his eyes once more. "Um, as a general rule, I don't kiss on the first date."

A smile appeared, slow and sexy. "Then we're in luck, because this sure as heck isn't a first date. It's more like an extended, recovering disaster of a first meeting."

Instead of the prolonged anticipation of his kiss increasing her anxiety, her tension eased with his teasing observation. She pretended to think about his description while his fingers gently massaged her neck. After a few seconds, she shook her head with a soft smile of false regret. "Unfortunately, I don't kiss on those, either."

His eyes narrowed. His smile remained, but he dropped his hand and pulled something from his pocket. "Good thing I've got a trump card."

She frowned at his handful of mangled, dark leaves until a holly berry identified the foliage as the mistletoe from the zoo. Laughter bubbled up inside her. "Oh my God, you stole Butch's mistletoe!"

"I didn't steal anything," Eric denied. "Santa gave me an early Christmas gift."

"Yeah, sure," she teased.

"First I'm a jerk, now I'm a thief and a liar?" he challenged.

"I didn't say that!"

"Butch gave me the mistletoe right after he suggested I drive you home."

Marissa glanced up at the mistletoe in his hand. The wonderful little leaves conjured the vivid memory of Eric's warm mouth on hers and erased her smiling doubt. She reached up to take the mistletoe from his grasp and twirled it between her thumb and forefinger. Resting her forearm on his shoulder while his hands settled on her hips, she stepped close and flattened her other hand against his chest. His heartbeat thundered beneath her fingers. She slid them up over his T-shirt to link with her other arm around his neck.

Their bodies made full contact; thighs, hips, chests. His eyes darkened to slate gray, and heat jolted straight to her core.

"Soo…what is it that you said in the golf cart?" she whispered in breathless anticipation.

His head lowered. "Mistletoe rules."

"And I remember something about it's bad luck if we don't kiss under the mistletoe?"

He leaned closer, his breath brushing her lips. "*Very* bad."

"Who made up that rule?"

His gaze locked on hers. "Seriously? You want that story now?"

She grinned and shook her head, then closed her eyes at the exact moment his lips met hers. It began as a duplicate of the kiss at the zoo, but with her overblown fears put into perspective and no need to fight her overwhelming attraction, Marissa wasn't about to let the privacy of the workshop go to waste.

She tightened her arms about his neck, pressed closer to his solid length, and parted her lips in blatant invitation. Eric accepted with a deep, stomach-fluttering groan, angling his head to slide his tongue against hers.

The lingering flavors of the wine they'd drank danced on her tastebuds; sweet vanilla, ripe black cherry and tantalizing spices. Pine registered, too. She dragged a ragged breath into her tight lungs.

Eric. All him, all male.

His red-hot heat intensified every flavor and scent. Or were her enhanced senses a result of the wildfire burning between them? Delving her fingers into his hair, as thick and soft as she'd imagined, she eagerly sought to explore the inside of his mouth as he had hers. His hands roamed every inch of her back and lower before he pressed her back against the doorjamb, his hips tight against hers.

Desire pulsed through her with every thrust of his tongue and suggestive movement of his hips. A low moan of pleasure vibrated her chest, yet she couldn't have said which of them uttered the sound.

He tore his mouth from hers, raising both hands to brush her hair back and cup her face while their gazes connected. "Mistletoe definitely rules."

She smiled. His thumb rubbed across her throbbing bottom lip, and she opened her mouth to nip at the rough pad. The retreating fire in his eyes burst back to life. It took nothing more than a gentle tug to bring his mouth down again.

The next time they came up for air, she buried her face in the warm crook of his neck. Their hearts thundered in sync against each other. "Mmm, you smell like pine."

"That's the workshop."

"No." She inhaled deeply against his heated skin when he bared her neck to graze his teeth across her skin. "I've noticed it off and on all day, and it's not the same as when I first walked in here. It's you."

"Sorry." He nipped the edge of her earlobe. His hot breath sent a delicious tremor rippling along her sensitized flesh before he moved on. "I worked a couple hours this morning before leaving to pick up Reese for school."

"Don't apologize, I like it." She drank in the scent that had warmed and strengthened in the height of their passion.

He kissed his way along her jaw, so she framed his face with her hands, holding him still while she dipped her chin to capture his lips with hers. Raw desire gave way for something more tender and yet equally arousing. They pulled back at the same time, breathing deep but not labored.

Marissa stared wide-eyed at Eric's stunned expression. An emotional connection thrummed in the air like she'd never felt before. Her chest bound so tight, drawing sufficient oxygen proved difficult, leaving behind a sensation of lightheaded intoxication that had nothing to do with the wine.

"Daad!"

Marissa blinked and dropped her arms at the same time Eric took a hasty step back.

"Moomm!" A second later Reese and Heather skidded to a stop on the workshop porch, flashlights bobbing in their hands. The two girls stared at the adults.

"Come on, Dad, when are we going to start the campfire?" Reese asked with a hint of a whine.

Marissa couldn't make herself look away from Eric. Their severed physical connection did nothing to diminish the emotional link still hovering between them. He cleared his throat and ran a hand through his hair before finally transferring his full attention to his daughter.

"Ah...how about right now?"

"Yeah! Let's go!" Reese dashed back the

108

way they'd come. Like the flip of a switch, she jerked to a stop and retraced her steps. Heather hadn't even had a chance to move. Reese aimed her flashlight down and leaned over to scoop something off the floor. She shook off the sawdust. "Oh, cool! Mistletoe."

She didn't question where it'd come from, just held it over Heather's head and kissed her on the cheek. The two erupted in giggles. A second later they sprinted across the lawn toward the bonfire pit. "Last one there has to kiss a toad!"

Marissa reached for her crutches before looking up at Eric, a little nervous, but mostly happier than she'd been in a very long time. He extended his arm with a smile that matched the emotions singing inside her heart. She used his strength for balance and handed him the crutches on the other side. Halfway across the yard, he halted with a snap of his fingers.

"I forgot matches." After a glance toward the occupied girls, he dropped a quick kiss on Marissa's lips and handed her the crutches. "I'll be right back."

He loped back to the house and up the porch

stairs by the time Marissa reached the girls. She found a comfortable seat by the fire pit and propped her foot up to ease the throbbing.

Eric returned with a stack of newspaper, matches to light the fire, the makings for s'mores, and a patio chair cushion. The latter he arranged under Marissa's ankle as Reese cupped her hand and whispered to Heather. When flames had engulfed the wadded newspaper to lick along surfaces of the tee-peed chunks of wood in the fire pit, Eric dragged a chair next to Marissa's and sat down with a relaxed sigh.

Reese and Heather slithered in between the chairs and faced Eric, each of their faces wreathed in a wide grin. Heather held out her hands, cupped one on top the other. Suppressed merriment threatened to escape from the girls at any moment. Marissa knew they were up to something, but hadn't been able to decipher any of their covert whispers.

The moment Heather lifted her top hand, a toad leapt onto Eric's chest.

"What the—!" He jumped back in his seat, sending the girls into a fit of hysterics. By the time they'd contained themselves, he held the toad above his chest, the amphibian's feet dangling.

It peed on him.

Marissa's amusement burst free so hard she snorted. Then she couldn't stop laughing for the life of her.

"Take this thing," Eric ordered as the toad let loose a couple of frantic chirps.

Reese shook her head. "You were the last one here."

"I—" Eric broke off with a reluctant chuckle. "Get outta here. I'm not kissing a toad."

Reese pulled a hand from behind her back. With a triumphant grin, she held the rapidly disintegrating sprig of mistletoe over the toad. Eric gave a bark of laughter as a few pieces of sawdust fell onto his chest. He swung his head in Marissa's direction, his expression an obvious plea for help.

She shook her head and managed to curb her mirth long enough to say, "Mistletoe rules."

Eric looked from Marissa, to Reese, to Heather, and finally, with a sigh of resignation, at the toad. "Does she have a name?"

The toad gave three indignant sounding chirps.

"Warts is a boy," Reese announced.

"Great."

Marissa's cheeks ached from her permanent grin. Eric brought the toad closer with a comical look of distaste, then laughed with the rest of them when Warts squeezed his eyes shut tight at the split-second touch of his lips.

While handing the toad back to Heather, Eric snatched the mistletoe from Reese's grasp with his free hand. In the blink of an eye, he sat up and held it above Marissa's head. The girls pointed and snickered but were smart enough to scamper a safe distance away.

"Hey!" she protested, trying to catch her breath from laughing so much.

Leaves floated down in front of her face and one berry dropped down the v-neck of her black shirt to lodge in her bra.

"I'm taking whatever I can get now that we have an audience again," Eric warned as he leaned in for another kiss.

She halted his forward movement long enough to wipe the toad cooties from his mouth, then partook in some child-friendly mistletoe mischief with a newfound affection for Christmas in July.

Epilogue

*E*ric wound his way through the crowd, aiming for the garbage can to toss empty coffee and hot chocolate cups. The mall teemed with holiday shoppers and fighting his way back to his girls wasn't exactly a walk at the zoo. But the effort was oh so worth it.

He paused to watch the three of them where they waited by the fudge shop. Whether dressed for business, or casual in jeans and a sweater like now, Marissa never failed to take his breath away. Next to her, with carbon-copy honey-blond hair and blue eyes, Heather was sure to be just as beautiful when she grew up, the lucky little girl. And Reese…well, he may be a little biased, but she was as perfect as an angel sent from heaven.

Someone bumped into him from behind. The person continued without looking up or even bothering with an apology.

"Happy Holidays," Eric offered with a smile before resuming his trek. He'd definitely been blessed over the last five months, so he'd be the last one to act like Scrooge.

Eric stepped up behind Marissa and wrapped his arms around her to rest his chin on her shoulder. "Anyone want dessert?"

Marissa turned her head with a positive, "Mmm," and he pressed a quick kiss to the corner of her mouth.

"Now or later?" he whispered.

"Both."

"I'll have a cookie, please," Heather said.

"Daaadd," Reese whined. "You said we could go see Santa now." She made it sound as if getting a treat would take hours instead of only two minutes.

Eric stepped back to pull some money from his pocket. "You want a cookie or not?"

She looked at the display case full of fudge, cookies and other treats. "Yeah."

When Eric paused and lifted his eyebrows,

she corrected her response with a small smile.

"Yes, please."

Five minutes later they took their place in the line to see Santa Claus. It didn't take long to understand why the wait was so long, even though it was only the weekend before Thanksgiving. The mall had gone all-out on the North Pole set-up, including real trees to give off a fragrant pine scent, fake snow falling gently in the background, and most impressive, a live reindeer stalled just to the left behind St. Nick so the antlered animal would be in all the pictures.

The girls munched their cookies and found something new every couple seconds to point out to each other or their parents. Five months and it still amazed him how little the two fought, especially since in August Nina had agreed to joint custody and they now spent a lot of time together.

"So what did Mark have to say when he called earlier?" Marissa asked as they shuffled along.

"He ETS's in two weeks and should be home a few days later."

"ETS?"

"Sorry—military speak for expiration term of service. Once they process all the paperwork, he'll be all set. He won't make it for Thanksgiving, but he'll be here for Christmas."

"It'll be nice to have him around more."

"So long as he behaves," Eric agreed, watching the kids in line ahead of them.

"Oh, come on. He's fun to flirt with, but you know you're the only man for me."

"And it better stay that way," he warned with a mock scowl.

"Always." She lifted her face for a kiss and it took some effort to keep the affection public-friendly. The look in her blue eyes promised him sinful dessert later. "I love you."

He threaded his fingers with hers and raised her hand to his lips. "I love you, too."

She kissed him again before leaning her head against his shoulder. As they inched along closer to the front, Eric found his attention drawn more often to the jolly, bearded man in the red velvet chair. A lady dressed as Mrs. Claus stepped over to adjust the man's hat before the next child took a seat on his lap. She paused to kiss his rosy cheek. The two shared a loving smile, and that's when it hit him why the man looked so familiar. A glance at the redheaded elf taking pictures cinched it.

Marissa had bent to pick up a stray mitten and when she straightened, Eric leaned close so the girls wouldn't hear. "Recognize Santa?"

She stared for a long moment.

"Check out Mrs. Claus," he suggested.

A smile curved her lips. "Judy."

"Yeah. I'm glad we get to see them again."

"Me, too." Marissa's grin told him they both remembered that first mistletoe kiss in Santa's cart at the zoo.

Reese was next in line, and she scampered up to Santa to make her requests. When Heather finished her turn, Santa Butch called them both back and set one on each knee.

"Janey," he said to the elf behind the camera, "get a picture with both these little darlin's. Mother, come over here with us, too."

Judy hugged Heather to her side while they all smiled for the camera. Butch winked at Eric and Marissa just before the flash. Eric nodded to Mrs. Claus as the girls slid off Santa's lap, and then stepped forward to shake the man's hand.

"Santa. Eric Riley—don't know if you remember us from this past—"

"I remember, boy, I ain't senile."

Eric chuckled and put an arm around Marissa. "Well, then, let me formally introduce you both to my wife, Marissa Riley."

Santa's brows disappeared under the trim of his hat. "You don't waste no time, do you?"

"No, Sir," Eric said with a chuckle. Judy admired the newly acquired diamonds on Marissa's left hand.

Heather sidled up next to Santa's knee. "Mom and Eric got married in October. Reese and me got to be flower girls."

Santa leaned forward, looking from one girl to the other. "And you were both beautiful."

Their eyes widened. Reese whispered, "How'd you know?"

"Same way I know if you've been naughty or nice. You girls keep up the good work, you hear?"

They both nodded with wide grins.

"We'd better let you get back to work,"

Marissa said, glancing back at the long line. "Thanks so much for everything. This is amazing, by the way." She indicated the North Pole scene surrounding them.

Judy beamed with pride. "Our granddaughter Janelle set everything up."

The short, cute photographer nodded her thanks, her red curls peeking from beneath the white trim on her green cap.

"Before we go, can I get your phone number?" Eric asked Judy. "I have a present for the two of you that I'd love to deliver before Christmas."

Reese giggled. "Daddy, that's backwards."

"She's right. I bring the presents, not the other way around," Butch scolded. "Though, it looks like my work with you two is done fer this year."

"Actually…" Marissa threaded her fingers with Eric's. "Santa, I have a request."

Butch insisted she sit on Santa's knee. Eric gave her a smiling frown of confusion, but she just settled down without releasing his hand. Her other palm pressed against her stomach.

"We wouldn't trade our girls for anything…"

She lifted her shining blue eyes from Santa to Eric. "...but I think it's time for a boy."

It took a moment for her words to register. Eric's grip slackened in shock. The camera flash jarred him from the momentary daze. He blinked toward a grinning Janelle, then focused on his wife.

"A baby? Already?" he asked in a stunned whisper.

She nodded, her smile more beautiful than he'd ever seen. Pulling her to her feet with a loud whoop that echoed off the mall ceiling, he swung her around in his arms. The girls crowded around the moment he stopped, so Eric stooped to lift both of them up for a family hug.

"Eric..."

Eric glanced over his shoulder at Butch. Santa winked, his white-gloved hand pointing above their heads. Familiar leaves and holly berries adorned an elaborately decorated arch. Eric gave a hearty laugh and met Marissa's twinkling eyes.

Then, because mistletoe ruled in their house, he gave each one of his girls an early Christmas kiss.

Thank you for reading!

If you enjoyed ***Mistletoe Mischief***, reviews are always greatly appreciated.

And you'll definitely want to check out the entire *USA Today Bestselling*

Romancing Wisconsin Series

To everything there is a season...

Love finds a way during the four seasons in the Romancing Wisconsin Series. Starting with the Christmas holiday/Winter, then moving on to Autumn, check out the first six books in this bestselling, heartwarming series set in small town Wisconsin. Meet the Rileys, the Walshes, and best of all, Butch...a.k.a. *Santa* Butch. The mischievous matchmaker makes a cameo in each story—adding a touch of magic to the lives of everyone he loves, and even those he's just met.

Romancing Wisconsin Series List
Mistletoe Mischief, book 1
Mistletoe Magic, book 2
Mistletoe Match-Up, book 3
   **Mistletoe Rules* – short bonus story available through newsletter sign-up
Autumn Wish, book 4
Autumn Bliss, book 5
Autumn Kiss, book 6
   **Autumn Glimmer* – short bonus story available through newsletter sign-up
Spring Fling, book 7
Spring Serendipity, book 8 (early 2016)

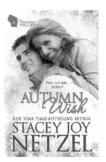

About the Author

I fell in love with books at a young age, and growing up, whenever Dad realized I'd disappeared when I was supposed to be working, he usually found me hiding out somewhere with a book. Writing evolved from reading, and the first story I ever finished was in high school, about my celebrity crush. I got an A on that creative writing 'assignment,' though I'm not sure my teacher ever read all 187 pages. I started writing again in my mid-twenties, and no matter the journey my characters take, the end result is always the same— Happily Ever After.

After years of being a travel agent while writing on the side, I am now able to live my dream of being a full time writer. I'm still an avid reader, and also a fan of movies with that HEA. I live in my native Wisconsin with my husband and kids, and in my limited free time, I enjoy gardening, canning, and visiting my parents in Northeastern Wisconsin (Up North) at the family cabin on the lake.

Check out my website at STACEYJOYNETZEL.COM to sign up for my Newsletter. Not only do subscribers receive new release updates, they also enjoy EXCLUSIVE contests, and bonus short stories to go along with my bestselling Romancing Wisconsin series.

~~~

Join Stacey Joy Netzel's Newsletter

http://bit.ly/SJNnewsletter

New release updates

Exclusive content

Contests and special sales

You can also find me online here:
Website and Blog:
http://www.StaceyJoyNetzel.com
Facebook: **Facebook.com/StaceyJoyNetzelAuthor**
Twitter: **http://twitter.com/StaceyJoyNetzel**

Hearing from readers is a very special thing for any writer, so feel free to contact me at any of the above locations.

~Thank you, and wishing you
many hours of happy reading!~
Stacey

Recommended Reads

For more heartwarming, small town romance read the *USA Today* bestselling **Welcome to Redemption Series** by Donna Marie Rogers and Stacey Joy Netzel.

...a small town in Northeast Wisconsin where second chances don't always come easy, but if you're willing to try, anything is possible.

"With their easy, breezy style and skilled characterizations, Rogers and Netzel have created a town that readers won't want to leave." ~ Romantic Times Book Reviews

"I felt like I lived in Redemption and knew everyone well. The stories kept getting better and better. So glad there is more to come. Can't wait!" ~ Amazon reviewer

"This is a great series - fell in love with the books, the characters and the town of Redemption. Read the first book and got hooked. Each book brings you deeper into the relationship of the citizens of Redemption, and you really begin to think of them as friends." ~ BN Reviewer

WELCOME TO REDEMPTION Series Order

Book 1: *A Fair Of The Heart*, **by Donna Marie Rogers**
Book 2: *A Fair To Remember*, **by Stacey Joy Netzel**
Book 3: *The Perfect Blend*, **by Donna Marie Rogers**
Book 4: *Grounds For Change*, **by Stacey Joy Netzel**
Book 5: *Home Is Where the Heart Is*,
        by Donna Marie Rogers
Book 6: *The Heart of the Matter*, **by Stacey Joy Netzel**
Book 7: *Never Let Me Go*, **by Donna Marie Rogers**
Book 8: *Hold On To Me*, **by Stacey Joy Netzel**
Book 9: *Say You Love Me*, **by Donna Marie Rogers**
Book 10: *Say You'll Marry Me*, **by Stacey Joy Netzel**

Italy Intrigue Series
Romantic Suspense

Her perfect vacation wasn't supposed to include kidnapping and murder.

Lost IN **ITALY**

ITALY INTRIGUE SERIES - 1

NEW YORK TIMES BESTSELLING AUTHOR
STACEY JOY NETZEL

Amazon Top 10 Bestseller
2012 Write Touch Readers' Award Winner,
Romantic Suspense

The best laid plans…

Television producer Halli Sanders is an obsessive planner. Not on the itinerary for her trip-of-a-lifetime to Italy? The disappearance of her siblings, dodging bullets, a high speed car chase, and being kidnapped by a sexy movie star. And that's just in the first three hours.

…often go awry…

A-lister Trent Tomlin put his career on hold to investigate his brother's suspicious death. When an American tourist unwittingly films the murder of the retired cop who's been helping him, Trent has no choice but to abscond with the woman and her dangerous movie. But the killers will stop at nothing to get the incriminating evidence—including hold Halli's family as collateral.

Life is a little different unscripted…

Thrust into the role of real-life hero, Trent finds himself falling for the Plain Jane whose beauty blossoms with every challenge they face. He needs the evidence to put the murderers behind bars. Halli needs it to rescue her siblings. Their attraction heats up, but unless they can find a way to work together, all the planning in the world won't guarantee a happy ending.

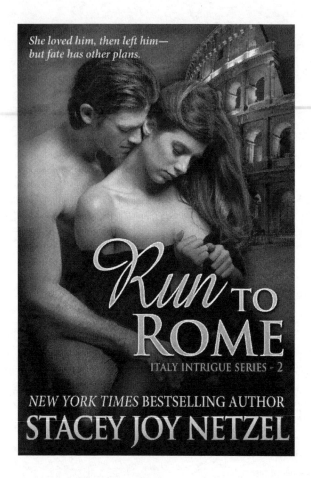

She loved him, then left him— but fate has other plans.

Run TO ROME

ITALY INTRIGUE SERIES - 2

NEW YORK TIMES BESTSELLING AUTHOR

STACEY JOY NETZEL

Love him and leave him.

Nine months ago, undercover detective, Ispettore Evalina Gallo, protected her heart the only way she knew how, never expecting to see her savior-turned-one-night-stand again. When he returns to *Italia*—now a person of interest in an investigation of a local organized crime family—her personal connection to the rugged

American gets her assigned to the case.

A second chance to make things right.
With his mother's pleas ringing in his ears, Ben Sanders plans to retrieve a stolen bible his father shipped to Italy thirteen years ago, and then get out as fast as he can. But with the arrival of the beautiful detective, he suspects his mother's desire to right past wrongs might not be the whole truth.

Destiny will not be denied.
Now, less than twenty-four hours after entering the country, he's getting shot at—again. In a race from Milan to Rome to find the precious book before anyone else, time is ticking for the one-time lovers. Attraction burns hotter than molten lava, but amid secrets and half-truths, they must learn to trust each other if they have any hope of a future together.

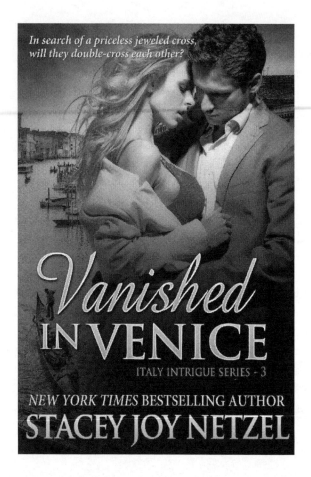

In search of a priceless jeweled cross,
will they double-cross each other?

Vanished
IN VENICE

ITALY INTRIGUE SERIES - 3

NEW YORK TIMES BESTSELLING AUTHOR
STACEY JOY NETZEL

*The cross is the key and hearts are on the line.
But can love survive a double-cross when the
mystery is unlocked?*

One year after being shot in Italy, Rachel
Sanders returns in search of the jeweled cross
that triggered a heartbreaking family betrayal.
Determined to keep the treasure from her

mother's greedy hands, she's caught off guard by the interference of an irresistibly charming rival. His unexpected offer to help might be self serving, but she's thrown into a precarious situation where she can't refuse...and finds she doesn't want to anyway.

Nick Marshall has a family legacy to recover and a score to settle. Anyone with the last name Sanders is fair game—until he meets Rachel. She's gorgeous, smart, sexy, and doesn't buy one word of his cover story. When their attraction combusts, each kiss makes his deception burn like acid, and he begins to question his end goal.

But they're not the only ones after the cross. Ruthless players willing to do anything to recover the treasure first put Nick and Rachel's lives on the line (in danger, at risk). Despite all the secrets and lies, lines quickly blur between the con and the real deal. Can love survive a double-cross when the mystery is unlocked?

Colorado Trust Series
Romantic Suspense

Evidence of Trust (book 1)
"This book grabbed me from the beginning and I couldn't put it down. I loved Britt and Joel! I loved the action and the suspense and of course the romance!!" ~ Angie, Amazon reviewer

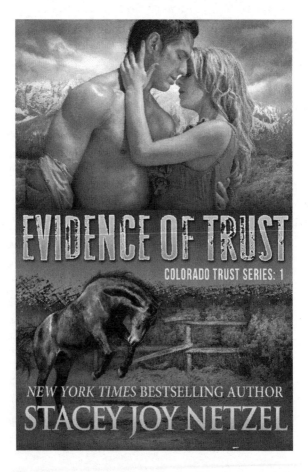

Having grown up under the excessive expectations of her CEO father, Brittany Lucas is as resistant to authority as the mustang she's training for her boss. It's a fault that lands her in more danger than she bargains for while camping in the back-country of the Rocky Mountain National Park.

Ranger Joel Morgan is used to having the upper hand in all his cases—until he runs into the headstrong blond while investigating disturbing incidents of poaching in the park. Brittany's imprudent lie of omission awakens ghosts in his past, making the sizzling attraction between them unwelcome.

As he searches for evidence he can trust her, the monster mutilating wildlife turns his sights on Brittany, and Joel discovers he'll do whatever it takes to protect her—even give his own life.

Trust by Design (book 2)

"Sizzling, sensual, spicy, sweet—Ms. Netzel dazzles her readers with a perfect romance in the midst of danger." ~ Casey Clifford, award winning romantic suspense author

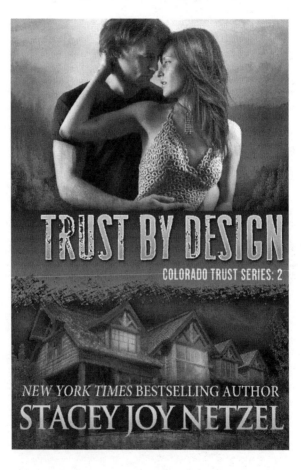

Cinderella and Prince Charming...brought together by chance, or design?

Interior Designer Gina Allen is flat broke thanks to a shady assistant who didn't pay the taxes. Now she has no choice but to accept a job from the very rich, very handsome CEO Dean Daley—even though he's accused her of conspiring to steal his software designs.

Keep your friends close and your enemies closer—that's why Dean hires his rival's ex-girlfriend. If he can use her to prove Jack is behind the spiraling downfall of his company, he might be able to turn things around before losing everything.

Dean, however, doesn't count on Gina being everything he never expected, or his heart being in more danger than his business. Will the trust they've built be enough to keep them together—or will an unexpected betrayal tear them apart...and possibly cost them their lives?

Trust in the Lawe (book 3)

*"I have a great respect for Stacey Joy Netzel
and the way she can write a romantic story with
sizzle and spice that kept me absolutely
addicted. To sum it all up, Outstanding book,
not to be missed."* ~ Val Pearson, You Gotta
Read Reviews, 5Stars

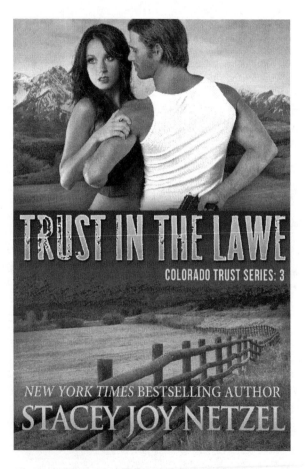

Kendra Zelner has three brothers: Eight-year old Noah she's determined to protect, Joel has no clue she exists, and Robert wants her dead.

With reason to be distrustful of cops, she takes Noah and flees their Manhattan home for Joel's ranch in Colorado. Under the pretense of needing a job, she plans to hide out until her twenty-fifth birthday, when she'll inherit her trust fund and legally gain custody of Noah away from Robert's greedy hands. Unfortunately, her new-found brother's sexy, infuriating ranch manager insists on demolishing her defenses and digging into her past.

Colton Lawe has good reason to suspect Joel's beautiful, long-lost sister isn't what she seems—the little liar stole from him! He silently vows to expose her secrets, but long hours together on the ranch fosters a friendship and attraction neither of them expects. Can Kendra trust Colton with the full truth before Robert tracks them down?

Shattered Trust (book 4)

"Shattered Trust has everything a fantastic book should have, romance, suspense, betrayal, and humor in all the right places." ~ Emily, Single Title Reviews

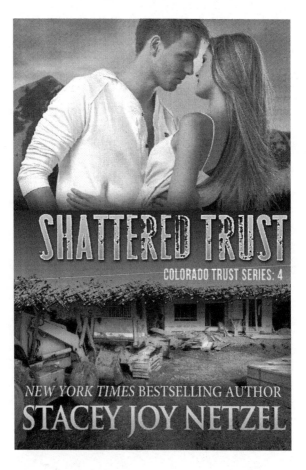

Sweet twenty-seven and never been kissed. Well...no one's ever accused Marley Wade of being sweet. Raised in the world of construction by a strict father, Marley knows what it takes to succeed as a general contractor in a man's world. The last thing she needs is an employee who makes her feel soft and feminine.

A new co-owner of Hunter Construction, Justin Blake goes undercover on Marley's crew to discover the truth behind his grandfather's death. But he didn't count on an instant attraction to his boss—or for it to develop into deeper emotions. When a blackmailer threatens to expose the twenty-five-year-old secrets that link his family and Marley's, Justin realizes the truth could not only shatter a future with her, but his entire family as well.

Dare to Trust (book 5)

"Thoroughly entertaining...I lost track of the time because I was so engrossed in the story." ~
Diana Coyle, Night Owl Reviews

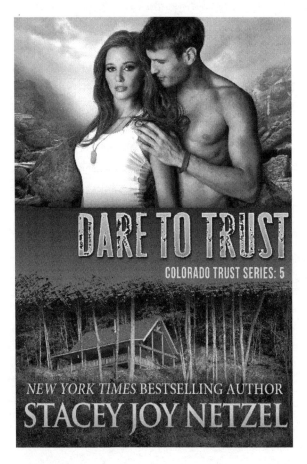

Ad-exec Jordan Blake believed image was everything—until his parents were convicted of murder, the family company went bankrupt, and his excessive drinking and arrest fueled the tabloids. When lawyer David Barnes offers representation in exchange for assistance in reopening his Colorado mountain resort, Jordan has no choice. It's help or jail.

Hollywood wild child Lexie Sinclair disappeared by changing her name, joining the army, and marrying a soldier. Then her husband wrapped their car around a tree, killing himself, and leaving her permanently injured. For the past few years, she's been content to live in peaceful obscurity as caretaker of David's defunct resort.

Jordan's arrival exposes Lexie's true identity and brings her dead husband's 'friends' calling. Jordan offers to help, but the shadow of his drinking leaves Lexie reluctant to trust. Can they conquer their fears and find the courage to face the criminals—and the world—together?

Made in the USA
Middletown, DE
08 October 2016